It was enough

seed of hope.

If she was unhappy then she could do something about it. If…no, *when* she escaped, Tim would be there for her.

He would always be there for her.

It was just as well the bright, flashing lights suddenly intruded into the dark compartment that had almost become a confessional, because otherwise Tim might have said something he shouldn't. Or, worse, done something he shouldn't—like take Kathryn in his arms and kiss her. He could almost imagine that she wanted him to do precisely that, because even the unwelcome brightness of the police car's beacons hadn't been enough to make Kathryn look away from him.

EMERGENCY RESPONSE

Doctors… Police... Fire... Ambulance...

Police officers and paramedics, nurses and fire officers: meet the dedicated men and women of the emergency services.

Every day is packed with drama as they race to help others. But while they're saving lives... they're finding love!

Mills & Boon® Medical Romance™ is proud to present

EMERGENCY RESPONSE—
the exciting new mini-series from Alison Roberts

The Recovery Assignment
The Firefighter's Baby
Emergency at Inglewood

EMERGENCY AT INGLEWOOD

BY

ALISON ROBERTS

MILLS & BOON®

First published in Great Britain 2004
Paperback edition 2005
Harlequin Mills & Boon Limited,
Eton House, 18-24 Paradise Road, Richmond, Surrey TW9 1SR

ISBN 0 263 84285 1

Set in Times Roman 10½ on 11¾ pt.
03-0205-51319

Printed and bound in Spain
by Litografia Rosés, S.A., Barcelona

CHAPTER ONE

HE WAS lying to her.

It was as obvious as the stain of colour that instantly heated Kathryn Mercer's cheeks, and her discomfort increased as the lie hung in the air between them. It was taking on a life of its own with a past history they shared, a present embarrassment they were both clearly experiencing and the shine taken off a future that Kathryn had been eagerly anticipating.

Was he trustworthy?

Kathryn deposited her small backpack with personal supplies for her first day at work in the allocated locker and took a little more time than she actually needed to push it securely into the small space and fold the strap ends away so they wouldn't catch in the door.

'That's about all there is in here.' Paramedic Tim McGrath was not looking at Kathryn as she stowed her bag. 'There's a shower and toilet through that door but it's unisex. If you want one that's women only you'll need to go upstairs to the bedroom area.'

A seed of resentment bloomed as she heard the echo of the lie.

'Sorry, I couldn't ring. I…lost your phone number.'

Kathryn shut the locker with a firm clang of metal on metal. It shouldn't be a big deal so why was she feeling so crushed? She'd only met Tim on that one occasion, months ago, in a situation that had been emotionally charged for everyone involved. What evidence had she really had to build such a picture of someone who could be trusted?

'Here's the office.' Tim was still avoiding eye contact as he led Kathryn away from the locker room. 'We have a separate area from the fire service for administration stuff. We share the commonroom and kitchen facilities, though.'

The let-down was refusing to fade. Kathryn had remembered Tim as some kind of hero—arriving at an emergency and taking charge calmly and skilfully. A professional picture impressive enough to have lured her into a new career. The desire to be like him had been strong enough to carry her through all the obstacles she had faced in changing jobs. And those obstacles had been enough to make it no small triumph that she was standing here today. No wonder her nervous excitement was making her over-sensitive.

A burst of deep male laughter could be heard well away from the small office as Kathryn nodded at various instructions she was being given about using the phone, fax machine and computer. Kathryn had arrived early for her first day at Inglewood station but a shift changeover was due shortly and there would be two fire crews and another ambulance crew somewhere on site. Possibly all male. Kathryn sucked in a deep breath to try and quell any nerves. Maybe Sean was right and she would find herself totally unsuitable for work like this.

Tim looked up at the sound of laughter and Kathryn thought she detected some relief in the knowledge they weren't alone in this old converted house. 'I'll introduce you to the mob if you're ready. We could grab a quick cup of coffee before we go and check the truck. Any questions so far?'

Harbouring a suspicion that he was untrustworthy was hardly the best way to break the ice with the man who would be her partner and hopefully her mentor for the next six months. Kathryn pushed a wayward tendril of blond hair behind her ear and smiled.

'Not right now but I'm sure I'll be a nuisance for the rest of the day. This is all so new.'

'You're a nurse, though, aren't you?' Tim glanced at the qualification patch on the sleeve of Kathryn's white shirt. 'Isn't that why you're already qualified for IV and cardiac procedures even though you're in a probationary position?'

Kathryn nodded. 'I worked in Emergency when I first qualified, but for the last few years I've been a part-time practice nurse in a general practice.' She pulled a wry face. 'My IV qualification is about the only skill I kept up. I seemed to spend half my time taking blood samples from geriatric patients who weren't exactly filled with the joys of living.'

'What made you decide to join the ambulance service?'

'You did.'

'You're kidding!'

Kathryn's smile widened as Tim visibly relaxed a little for the first time and advertised his interest in the conversation by perching one hip on the corner of the desk. 'No, I'm perfectly serious. I was out of my depth that day I met you, looking after a woman who was obviously very sick. The relief when you guys came and took over was amazing, and watching you work made me realise how much I'd like to be able to really help in a situation like that.'

'You did help. And you'd done all the right things before we got there, laying her down and taking some baseline vital signs. You were great.' Tim smiled back at her.

'Was she a triple-A, like you thought?'

An eyebrow lifted. 'You've got a good memory. That was months ago.'

'It made a big impression on me. Enough to make me apply for a career in the ambulance service. And I've always wondered how she got on. I watched the paper for a few days but I didn't see a death notice.'

Tim shifted, looking uncomfortable again at the reminder of not keeping his promise to ring Kathryn and let her know the patient outcome. 'She didn't die but it was touch and go there for a while. It *was* a rupture of an abdominal aortic aneurysm. They got her into Theatre almost immediately and fixed the rupture and dissection with a graft. She was fine.' He stood up. 'I'm sorry I couldn't let you know at the time.'

'Doesn't matter.' Kathryn watched as Tim headed for the door. It did matter, though. Enough to make her pursue the issue just a little further. '*I* should have rung *you*,' she added. 'An empty syringe package wasn't exactly the best place to write my phone number.'

Tim shrugged. 'I guess not,' he agreed, a shade too readily. 'Bit too easy for it to disappear along with the rest of the rubbish.'

So he'd thrown it away. That he was being truthful about the package going into the rubbish was as obvious as the lie about losing it had been. Kathryn followed Tim along the corridor to the source of the buzz of male conversation and laughter.

She was missing something here and her instincts told her it was something significant. What she couldn't understand was *why* it was important enough to be difficult to lie about. Or was Tim McGrath normally so honest that he had trouble with any fabrication? Kathryn hoped that was the case but only time would tell.

Entering the commonroom was daunting. The group of men was seated around a long dining table and their breakfasts were abandoned as Tim walked towards them.

'This is Kathryn Mercer,' he told the group. 'But she prefers to be called Kat. She's Laura's replacement on Green Watch for the next six months.'

The chorus of greetings was friendly.

'Have some porridge, Kat,' someone suggested. 'Mrs Mack always makes enough to feed an army.'

'Um…thanks, but I already had breakfast.' Actually, Kathryn had been feeling far too sick from nerves to eat anything so far today, but there was no way she could face porridge even on the best of mornings.

'So did I.' Tim flashed her the ghost of a wink. 'All the more for you guys. Have a second helping, Stick.'

One of the firemen muttered something inaudible and a small, wiry figure emerged from the kitchen area.

'That's enough o' that muttering, Jason Halliday. Porridge is good for you. It's the only thing that puts a good lining on your stomach on these cold mornings.'

'This is Kathryn, Mrs Mack,' Tim said. 'My new partner. Kat, this is Jean McKendry, who lives next door and is kind enough to spend her days looking after Inglewood station.'

Kathryn smiled. The woman reminded her of her grandmother and she could see the warmth that lay below the stern tone. 'Hi,' she said shyly.

'Och, but she's just a wee thing.' Kathryn was subjected to a concerned frown over half-moon spectacles. 'How's she going to cope in with this lot?' The older woman sniffed and Kathryn had the horrible feeling that her competence was in as much doubt as her physical ability to handle a demanding job. Then Jean McKendry sniffed even more pointedly, muttered something about muffins burning and disappeared back into the kitchen on an apparently urgent mission.

The blond fireman, Jason, was grinning. 'Kat's little and she's blond. Tim's big and brown. What does that remind you of, Stick?'

'Laura isn't exactly tall, Jase.'

'No, but my Laura's got a bit of meat on her bones.' Jason

shook his head impatiently. 'Come on…it's not rocket science. What are we eating here?'

More than one of his colleagues was grinning. The rest were looking blank.

'Porridge,' Jason said with a grimace. He cast a somewhat guilty glance towards the kitchen but dealing with the muffins was obviously keeping the housekeeper out of earshot and his grin appeared again. 'Come and sit down, Goldilocks.'

Kathryn laughed. She liked this fireman and she liked the fact that she was already being accepted enough to earn a nickname. She stole a glance at her partner. He *was* rather bear-like. Tall and solid with brown hair and brown eyes. Not at all fierce, though. He seemed to be enjoying the exchange as much as Kathryn, and his smile was the most genuine she had seen so far.

'We need to go and check the truck,' Tim said, after a glance at the wall clock. 'We'll get a coffee after that if it's still quiet so you'll get a chance to talk to Kathryn later.' He turned towards her and his smile became simply polite. 'These guys don't have to work nearly as hard as we do. They spend most of their days sitting around drinking coffee and talking. Just don't believe everything they tell you.'

'We get bacon and eggs for breakfast in summer,' one of them said.

'That *is* true.' Tim's gaze veered towards the kitchen but there was no sign of the porridge-maker. He lowered his voice anyway. 'Roll on summer!'

The appreciative chuckle followed the two ambulance officers as they left the commonroom. Clearly Tim was far more relaxed with this group of men than he was with her but that was hardly surprising. They didn't know each other and they had started their acquaintance with Tim's astonished recognition of Kathryn as the member of the public who had assisted a woman in trouble in a restaurant, rapidly followed by his unsuccessful attempt to cover up why he hadn't bothered to phone her.

At least he had recognised her. It would have been even more of a let-down to find she had made no impression on the man who had been in her thoughts with astonishing frequency over the last few months.

She followed Tim towards the garage where the fire engine and ambulance were parked. Let it go, she told herself firmly. It really doesn't matter that he didn't ring you. He probably just got busy with another emergency and forgot. Perfectly reasonable if that was the case, but why hadn't he just said so?

The outgoing crew was happy to hand over their pagers and head home for some sleep.

'Good luck,' they told Kathryn. 'And just tell Tim to shut up when you get sick of him talking all the time.'

Kathryn raised an eyebrow and Tim smiled wryly. 'I'm known for being a bit on the quiet side,' he explained. 'You're more likely to get bored stiff with my company than sick of listening to me talking.'

'I doubt very much that I'll get bored,' Kathryn told him. 'You might need to tell *me* to shut up if I ask too many questions.'

'I'm happy to answer anything I can. That's part of what taking on a probationary officer is all about.' Tim handed Kathryn a paging device and showed her how to scroll through messages.

'The job number and date come up first. Then the priority for the call. P1 is a life-threatening emergency and the only one we use lights and sirens for. P2 is non-urgent but requires a response time of less than thirty minutes, and P3 is routine stuff like inter-hospital transfers. P4 is a private hire.'

'What sort of reasons do people hire an ambulance for?'

'To take a relative back to a rest home or hospice after they've had a few days at home maybe. Usually it's a rest home bringing a resident back after they've been checked out after a fall or something.'

'OK.' Kathryn nodded, tucking the information away. P1s were going to be the calls she would be most nervous about.

The thought of heading off to an unknown emergency with the wail of a siren distracting her from remembering even well-rehearsed protocols was enough to make the back of her neck prickle. Thank goodness she had someone like Tim McGrath for a partner. He looked to be in his mid-thirties and had the aura of a relaxed attitude to his job that could only come from a combination of competence and experience.

Kathryn had also had the advantage of seeing Tim in action thanks to that incident in the restaurant. She knew he was competent and could stay calm in an emergency. She'd be OK with a partner like Tim. Becoming good at this job wasn't just a fantasy. She *could* do it.

'Of course, dispatch can only make a priority decision based on the information *they* get given,' Tim continued thoughtfully. 'Quite often a P1 is nothing significant, but you can get some of the sickest people on a P2.'

Kathryn chewed her bottom lip as the flash of confidence faded. She'd have to worry about both P1s *and* P2s, then.

Tim's amused expression made her flush with embarrassment at showing obvious nerves, but his smile was reassuring. 'They get it right most of the time. Like that restaurant case you were involved in. Having got the job definition on the pager as ''abdo pain'' at a restaurant, we thought we were going to a case of food poisoning and thought the P1 response was a bit of overkill. Turned out it *was* a life-threatening emergency, wasn't it?'

'I've never been more relieved in my life than I was when I heard that siren getting closer,' Kathryn confessed. 'I could tell she was really sick and I had no idea why. A heart attack seemed the most likely cause but the abdominal pain didn't exactly fit.'

'Some MIs do present with epigastric or back pain so it wasn't so far off the mark for a diagnosis. At least you knew how important it was to get urgent help.'

'And at least I know a bit more about triple-As now. I paid particular attention to that lecture.'

'So tell me, then.' Tim leaned against the back doors of the ambulance, swinging his pager by the curly elastic cord attached to a clip. The awkwardness of revisiting that particular case seemed to be receding and he was obviously warming to his new role as a mentor. 'What *do* you know about triple-As?'

A chance to impress Tim was welcome. Maybe he was uncomfortable with her because he had no idea what she was capable of. 'The signs are a pulsating mass in the abdomen and you might hear a bruit over the mass. If they rupture, it's a medical emergency. Signs and symptoms include a severe, tearing pain and blood loss leading to shock.'

'Causes?'

'Usually arterial disease. You can get a false aneurysm caused by trauma.'

'Do you know why the heart rate can stay normal?'

Kathryn frowned. 'I don't think we covered that in class…unless I've just forgotten.' She chewed her lip again. So much for impressing her new partner. 'With shock associated with blood loss you'd expect a tachycardia, wouldn't you? Seeing as that's the compensatory mechanism to try and keep the blood pressure up.'

Tim nodded, seemingly not bothered by any lack in her knowledge base. 'That's why it's such a good marker for a triple-A. An aneurysm causes the walls of an artery to bulge. When the aorta gets stretched it stimulates receptors into thinking that the blood pressure is actually high. Therefore the compensatory mechanism is to reduce the heart rate to keep the blood pressure down.'

'Not good for hypovolaemic shock.' Kathryn was delighted to have something explained so simply. Tim was obviously a good teacher and some of the excitement at the prospect of working with him returned to lift her spirits. 'And no wonder she started to feel better lying down with her feet up and then fainted when she sat up again.'

'Two litres of saline got the pressure up enough for us to be able to give her some morphine. She wasn't feeling too bad at all by the time we got her out of the restaurant. In fact, she was asking for you. She wanted to thank you.'

The awkwardness concerning the case returned with a rush, although it wasn't Tim's failure to phone her that was the cause this time. Kathryn found herself mirroring Tim's earlier action and fiddling with her own pager's safety cord.

'I...couldn't stay any longer.' She hoped Tim's memories of that evening were less clear than her own. Sean's patent ill humour at her involving herself in the case had been humiliating enough at the time.

'I hope your evening wasn't entirely ruined.'

The odd tone of the comment made Kathryn glance up in surprise, and she caught an expression she had no hope of reading in Tim's gaze. She needed to get him off any track concerning her personal life so she smiled brightly.

'Heck, no! That was the most exciting thing I'd done in years. It was what persuaded me to throw in my practice nurse job and train as an ambulance officer.'

'And is your...husband happy about it?'

'Sean?' Kathryn looked away, trying to sound casual and ignoring the odd hesitation in Tim's query. He wasn't to know how laughable the notion of her being out to dinner with anyone other than her husband was. It was laughable enough to make her smile again. 'He'll cope.'

She was unaware of the defiant tilt her chin adopted. He'd have to cope. There was no way he was going to interfere with her new career. Even mentioning Sean had added a new tension to the atmosphere and Kathryn's shiver had little to do with the chilliness of the garage they were standing in.

Care was going to be needed in future not to allow any mention of her home life to intrude on her work hours. This career was her hope for the future. An escape. Something Sean had no part of, and she intended to keep it that way despite the clutch of any tentacles of guilt. Most importantly, she didn't want Tim or anyone else at Inglewood station knowing anything about her marriage.

If you could even call it that.

Fortunately, Tim seemed completely uninterested. He snapped his pager into the holder clipped to his belt and Kathryn followed his example.

'There are other priorities as well.' His tone was coolly professional once again. 'At times we're on standby for fires or armed offender callouts for the police, long-distance transfers and back-up assistance for other ambos. You'll pick it all up in no time.'

'I hope so.' Kathryn watched Tim open a side door of the ambulance.

'Here we have the ramps, carry chair, hare traction splint and KED. Have you covered using the KED?'

Kathryn nodded. Her class had been through more than one scenario training them to use the body splint to help extricate car accident victims. Having to attend a major car crash on her first day was a prospect that had kept her awake for a large part of the previous night. The image of trying to cope with such a scene took turns with an even greater fear—that she might have to defibrillate someone for the first time.

When the side door refused to close easily, Tim took a few minutes to rearrange the contents. Kathryn watched him, aware that her fears about what the day might bring and what would be revealed about her competence paled in comparison to a much darker fear that Tim had inadvertently reminded her of. A fear that had presented one of the largest obstacles to her career change.

Tucked away in her boring job as a GP nurse in an old-fashioned clinic in the suburbs had been safe. It had been easy to keep up the pretence of a happy marriage with the elderly GP who had been a close friend of Sean's father because he hadn't been any more interested in Kathryn than he was in his patients. Old Dr Braithwaite had been far too busy having an affair with the clinic's receptionist and Kathryn had been forced to turn a blind eye because she knew, better than anyone, that it wasn't always the husband's fault. It was quite possible for a totally inadequate wife to drive a man into the arms of another woman. A whole string of them, even.

And here she was taking on a career she was determined to excel in, which meant she would be working with a lot of men. Inglewood station was a peripheral city response base that housed both fire and ambulance crews, and being assigned here accentuated the difference in the age group and numbers of her new colleagues. She was going to be in almost daily contact with a lot of men who would inevitably be very sympathetic to Sean…if they knew. Kathryn would end up being labelled in terms she couldn't bear to imagine, even if there was justification in such derision.

Her problems had nothing to do with life on the outside, however. An 'outside' that was now a new start. The future had always been haunted by the unknown but for the first time in many years some of those unknowns were exciting. Compelling, even. Kathryn had taken the first brave steps on a solo journey she had every intention of continuing.

Straightening her spine, she caught one of the swinging doors as Tim opened up the back of the ambulance and she pushed it to catch in the open position.

'Are you comfortable with the layout and finding what you need in here?'

She nodded confidently. 'That's something I *can* do.'

'Right. Quick test, then.' Tim vaulted into the back of the ambulance, surprisingly lightly for such a big man. He tapped the sliding glass door of an overhead locker. 'What's in here?'

'Straps for the scoop stretcher or backboard, hard hat, cervical collars, maternity kit and incontinence pads.'

Tim grinned. 'Let's hope we don't need too many of those on your first day. And this one?' He tapped another locker on the opposite side of the truck.

'Dressings in three sizes, bandages—also in three sizes—saline pouches, triangular bandages and another hard hat.'

'Where's the IV gear?'

'In the drawer under the life pack.' Thoughts of Sean or fears of her private life being exposed were mercifully fading into oblivion. This was fun.

'And?'

Taken aback, Kathryn frowned as her gaze raked the remaining storage spaces. 'Well…the giving sets and pressure cuff and bags of saline are in that locker over there and…um…'

'What happens if we need to put an IV line in when we're not in the back of the truck?'

'Oh-h.' Kathryn rolled her eyes at her obvious omission. 'There's supplies of everything in the resuscitation kit.'

'Good.' Tim touched the large, tackle-type box with his foot. 'We'll go over the kit later. Are you familiar with this type of life pack?'

Kathryn nodded. 'That's what we've been using for training.'

'You're qualified to defibrillate manually, aren't you?'

Her nod was a lot slower this time. 'I haven't done it for real yet. Only on dummies.'

Tim's smile was quick. 'We'll try and make sure your first arrest patient isn't too bright, then.'

Kathryn laughed but was disconcerted at the way Tim's gaze veered instantly away from her face. A slightly awkward silence fell, which added to Kathryn's confusion. This was like a roller-coaster. Whenever she felt that Tim was being friendly and they were establishing some kind of rapport, it got flicked off like a switch and that inexplicable tension was back again. Had she done the wrong thing by laughing at his joke? Why had he made one if she wasn't supposed to find it funny?

Recognising that she was doing something wrong was a skill Kathryn was expert in, however. She cleared her throat. 'It must be a pain, having to work with someone like me.'

'What?' Tim snapped the battery he was checking back into its slot in the life pack.

'I mean, I must seem a bit of a liability when you're used to working with someone as qualified as your last partner. Laura, was it?'

Tim nodded. 'Laura Green. Now Laura Halliday.'

'Halliday? Wasn't that the name of one of the firemen?'

Tim nodded again. 'Jason. He and Laura got married a few months ago. She's taking maternity leave now.'

'Oh.' Kathryn knew her smile was probably wistful. 'That's nice.'

'Yeah.' Tim clipped the safety belt that held the life pack

in position. 'She thinks so.' He looked directly at Kathryn. 'I hope I'm not giving the impression that I'm not happy to work with you. It's actually a bit of a treat, getting a probationary officer with your qualifications. I was expecting somebody as green as grass, which can make life a bit difficult for a while.'

'I'm still green,' Kathryn warned. 'As I said, it's been years since I worked in Emergency and all the pre-hospital emergency medicine I've learned over the last few months is still just theory.'

'You've done third crewing, though, haven't you?'

'It's not the same when you've got people walking you through stuff. It's a big step being out on the road as a qualified officer.'

'You'll learn soon enough,' Tim assured her. His eyebrows rose as their pagers sounded simultaneously. 'Perhaps even sooner than I thought. All set?'

'As long as I don't have to defibrillate someone on my first job.' Kathryn's smile was rather shaky as she climbed up into the passenger seat of the ambulance. Any concerns over the difficulty she was having breaking the ice with Tim fled into the same space Sean was now occupying.

Her pager informed her that this job was a P1 and it was already as nerve-racking as she had feared.

The switch to change the wail of the siren to a shorter yelp for additional warning at intersections was just above Tim's head. He left it on yelp and added a blast on the air horn for good measure when a courier van driver decided he could scoot past the other traffic already slowing obediently to give the emergency vehicle right of way. The driver's non-verbal sign that he wasn't impressed with being reprimanded drew a disgusted snort from Tim and a squeak from his new partner.

'Can you believe that guy?'

'Believe anything if it's a courier van,' Tim growled. 'Or a taxi. Or one of those little granny wagon boxes on wheels.' He could see Kathryn's hand shaking slightly as she tried to find the address they'd been given on the map. 'Don't worry,' he said shortly. 'I know where it is.'

His mood slipped another notch or two as he heard his tone. He should be giving Kathryn some encouragement, not making her feel as though he couldn't be bothered with any incompetence. This was her first day on the job, for heaven's sake, and as far as potential partners went he had probably scooped the pick of the latest intake. It would be nice to blame his uncharacteristic ill humour on the idiocy of courier van drivers but, sadly, Tim knew that he had been thrown off his usual even keel well before that.

About the time Kathryn Mercer had walked into the garage at Inglewood station this morning, in fact.

He must have looked like more of an idiot than a courier van driver with his mouth hanging open, but seeing Kathryn had been a shock to say the least. She was supposed to be firmly in the realms of fantasy now. Locked away like an attractive movie star. Perfect but totally unattainable. She wasn't supposed to walk into his life like that. How the hell could he be expected to work with someone he shouldn't have been thinking about in the kind of terms he had been?

Tim accelerated hard as he took a bend into a straight stretch of the main road leading to the Hutt Valley. Weaving in and out of the traffic didn't allow him time for more than a split-second glance at Kathryn but it was enough to absorb the impression of a white face and fingernails buried in the unforgiving upholstery of her seat. She was being thrown in the deep end here and Tim didn't like the tiny flash of satisfaction it gave him.

He was in control again and it felt like the first time since the sight of her diminutive figure in its smart new uniform had assaulted his senses. He had been the one out of his depth then, and he had really thought he'd been drowning when she'd said she'd been disappointed he hadn't kept his promise to ring her.

It should have been easy to lie and say the number scribbled on that empty syringe packet had been mislaid, or that they just got incredibly busy and he had forgotten. But he hadn't forgotten, had he? That moment of panic when he'd thought he'd lost the damn packet, the relief with which he'd fished it out of his pocket, and then the crushing disappointment as Laura had pointed out that both Kathryn and her dinner partner had been wearing wedding rings were burned into his memory with astonishing clarity.

The woman of his dreams, he'd confessed to Laura. And he'd been too late. Someone had got there first and claimed the kind of commitment that was sacrosanct as far as Tim was concerned. He should have been able to put any attraction in the rubbish along with that phone number, but that had proved impossible. As impossible as sounding casual enough to make a lie convincing.

It might have been OK if he'd had a little warning, but the change in Laura's replacement had only been decided that morning and Kathryn had arrived before he'd had time to collect any messages. He had still been trying to come to terms with the fact that he would be working closely with Kathryn for the next six months when she'd reminded him of precisely why that was going to be so awkward.

Tim pushed his foot down on the brake and Kathryn shot forward into the clutch of her safety belt.

'This is Rawlston Street. What number do we want?'

Kathryn sat back and fumbled for her pager.

'You should write that information on the case report

form as soon as we get a call,' Tim told her. 'You can't afford to waste any time if it's an emergency response.'

'Sorry.' Kathryn was pushing the button on her pager. 'It's number 257 and it says ''Fresh''.'

'Fresh Is Best. It's a supermarket up the end of the road.' Tim turned off the siren but left the beacons flashing as he slowed the ambulance. 'It's a chest pain,' he reminded Kathryn, 'so we'll take everything. Throw the life pack onto the stretcher along with the oxygen and suction kit. I'll get the kit. Let's move.'

CHAPTER TWO

ANXIOUS-LOOKING people wearing hats and white aprons over striped uniforms were waiting. Tim jumped out from the driver's seat and strode to the back to open the doors. Kathryn stayed inside the vehicle, sliding between the front seats into the back and struggling to unclip the safety belt on the life pack quickly. She could hear snatches of the information Tim was being given.

'Lifting sacks of flour. They're as heavy as…'

'Looks awful. All grey and sweaty…'

'Fifty-six. Never had a sick day in his…'

By the time Kathryn had the life pack on top of the stretcher, Tim had added all the other equipment they needed, unhooked the end of the stretcher and was pulling it free. Kathryn made a lunge to catch the handle on her end so it wouldn't crash down the steps. Then she had to trot to keep up.

Their patient *did* look awful. The middle-aged man was slumped against a wall near the massive ovens in the supermarket bakery.

'Get some oxygen on him,' Tim instructed Kathryn. 'Fifteen litres a minute with a non-rebreather mask.'

An easy enough task. Kathryn unzipped the pouch attached to the portable oxygen cylinder and ripped open a plastic bag containing a mask, only to find it was a standard acute mask. She reached into the bag again and this time found the one with the reservoir bag attached. She hooked it up to the cylinder and remembered to keep her finger over the hole at the base of the mask until the reservoir bag was full.

Tim had cut away the apron and uniform shirt of the man and was attaching the sticky electrodes on the ends of the life-pack leads.

'Have you got any history of heart problems?'

Their patient couldn't speak. Clearly in agonising pain, he clutched his chest and shook his head as he moaned incoherently.

Kathryn moved closer. 'I'm just going to put a mask on your face, sir,' she said. 'Is that OK?'

Patient consent was not forthcoming but Kathryn found her nervousness vanishing as she touched the man. She could do this. Without being told, she picked up the blood-pressure cuff and wrapped it round the man's arm. She listened with a stethoscope as she let the pressure in the cuff down but could hear nothing. Frowning, she caught Tim's gaze as he reached into the kit for a tourniquet.

'Unrecordable?' Tim mirrored Kathryn's quick nod. 'I'm not surprised. I couldn't get a radial pulse.'

That meant the man's systolic blood pressure was less than 80. Kathryn looked at the screen of the life pack and felt a chill of premonition. The trace looked far from normal with the spike of the QRS bizarrely wide.

'Complete heart block,' Tim said quietly. 'Draw me up a flush, would you, please, Kathryn? And give him an aspirin.'

Kathryn found her brain was moving far more quickly than her hands. Her fingers shook as she followed Tim's calm directions but she managed to draw up the morphine and other drugs he requested. There was no time to do anything more than absorb the impression of urgency after that as bakery staff helped get the man onto the stretcher and load him and the gear into the ambulance. Within a matter of minutes Kathryn found herself driving the ambulance towards the hospital with Tim in the back, caring for a very sick cardiac patient.

Driving such a large, heavy vehicle had been a challenge in itself during her training and it would be months before Kathryn would be allowed to drive under lights and sirens, but she was confident enough at road speed and far happier leaving Tim to care for the patient this time.

By the time they got back to the main road she was almost enjoying herself. Her first job with Tim had gone well, all things considered. Maybe she had been a bit slow drawing up the morphine and adding the saline, but she just wasn't used to doing things under such pressure of time. She'd get used to it soon enough. Pulling out the wrong oxygen mask had wasted valuable seconds, though. She'd have to—

'Pull over!' The shout from the back cut through any satisfaction enveloping Kathryn.

She checked the side mirrors and indicated that she was pulling onto the shoulder of the road.

'*Now*, Kat!'

She jammed on the brakes and heard a curse from Tim as he had to catch his balance.

'Get in the back,' Tim said tersely, as he reached for the radio microphone. 'Get the gel pads and charge up the defib. He's in VF.'

Oh…God! This was her worst nightmare. Her first job and she was expected to defibrillate someone. Kathryn could feel the prickle of perspiration break out down the entire length of her spine as she ripped open the foil packet and slapped two rectangles of spongy orange material onto the patient's chest.

'Charge it,' Tim snapped as a response to his radio signal

came through. 'We need back-up,' he told the control room. 'VF arrest.' He was watching Kathryn as he spoke.

She held a paddle in each hand. The crescendo of sound that depressing the charge button had elicited stopped with a loud beep. The paddles were charged.

'Do it,' Tim commanded.

Kathryn pressed the paddles onto the gel pads. She remembered to move so that her legs were not touching the metal sides of the stretcher. A flash of some horror story of an ambulance officer giving himself a nasty shock surfaced.

'I'm clear,' she said shakily. 'Are you?'

'Just *do* it, Kat!'

She pressed her thumbs down hard on the buttons. The man jerked and his arm flopped over the side of the stretcher to hit her leg. Kathryn lifted the paddles hurriedly, too horrified to look at the screen behind her.

'Charge again,' Tim ordered.

The sound started to crescendo again. Kathryn's clutch on the paddle handles felt slippery so she tightened her grip. Two shocks at 200 joules, she reminded herself. Then one at 360. Then CPR. She pressed the paddles into position.

'Wait!' Tim shouted. 'Look at the screen.'

Kathryn's head jerked up. A rapid but normal cardiac rhythm was evident. And here she was with charged-up paddles pressed onto the patient's chest. She lifted them and her jaw dropped. The only thing she could remember was how dangerous it was to discharge a shock into the air. She couldn't catch Tim's eye, though, as he was leaning past her. Hitting a button on the centre of the menu control dial… emptying the charge safely from the paddles.

He was talking into the microphone at the same time. 'Cancel the back-up,' he told Control. 'My partner has just saved our patient.'

Kathryn's jaw dropped even further. Was he *serious*?

'You can put those down now,' Tim said. Then he grinned. 'So, how does it feel to save a life, then?'

'I…ah…' Kathryn was totally lost for words. She looked at the patient who was actually moving his head and groaning. She looked at the life-pack screen, which still showed a rapid, steady sinus rhythm. Then she looked at Tim and couldn't help the grin that broke out.

'Now, let's see how fast you can get us into hospital,' Tim said. 'Use the lights and siren.'

'But I'm not allowed—'

'Just do it, Kat. This man's not exactly stable yet. Or would you rather stay in the back with him?'

Kathryn drove. She could see the reflection of the flashing beacons on the windows of vehicles she shot past. She found the wail of the siren became just a background as she concentrated hard on getting through the traffic. She even remembered to use the yelp switch at intersections. And she backed up to the loading ramp at the emergency department and managed to stop with only a gentle bump against the edge.

The resus team staff were waiting. Kathryn leapt out, opened the back doors and unhooked the foot end of the stretcher. Their patient was still hooked up to the life pack and oxygen as they wheeled him inside. He was sitting up now, though, and Kathryn couldn't believe it when he smiled at her.

'Thanks, love,' he said. 'I'm feeling a hell of a lot better now.'

So was Kathryn. The worst had happened and she had coped. Her first job and she had saved a life. *They* had saved a life. Kathryn's smile when Tim came out to help her clean up the truck was wide enough to let him know just how incredible the experience had been. She had been so right in fighting for the chance to do this job, and right now she was so happy it was all she could do not to throw herself into Tim's arms and dance along the loading ramp of the ambulance bay.

She was positively beaming at him. Tim had taken a few minutes to complete the paperwork inside so Kathryn had gone out to start the clean-up alone. And here she was, lit up like the happiest Christmas tree ever. Tim could understand how she felt. He could remember the first time he successfully defibrillated someone and the amazing satisfaction in getting them back. It didn't happen nearly often enough, and Kathryn was looking at him as though he'd arranged all this as a special gift to mark her first day at work.

Good grief. She looked as though she might actually give him a hug or a kiss or something. Tim stepped back hurriedly. Fantasy was much safer. He'd never factored in that electric current that Kathryn seemed to generate around herself. He had remembered her looks well enough—the colour and curl of her blond hair, the cute upturned nose, the wide blue eyes with that hint of anxiety. He hadn't seen her smile during that first encounter, however, and that seemed to be what was generating the current.

'All done?'

'Almost.' Kathryn bit her lip, clearly trying to control her smile. 'He thanked me, Tim, can you believe that? He looked dead only a few minutes ago and there he was sitting up and saying thank you.'

'You did a great job,' Tim said warmly. 'Well done.'

'We saved someone, didn't we, Tim?' Kathryn gave a tiny wriggle, like an overjoyed puppy. 'We really saved someone.'

'Yeah.' Tim couldn't prevent his own grin. 'Don't expect me to lay on a case like that every day, though. Consider it a ''welcome to Inglewood'' job.' Grabbing the pile of dirty linen from the floor, he turned away. What was he saying? He didn't want to welcome Kathryn to Inglewood.

What he really wanted was to ring the ambulance training manager and request a transfer of his probationary assistant. Yeah...right. Tim snorted as he shoved the linen into the bag inside the emergency department doors. Kathryn was lacking in confidence quite enough. He could never be so cruel as to let her think she wasn't up to scratch as far as he was concerned.

What could he say, anyway? Sorry, but I really fancy this chick and she's married to someone else so it's kind of like letting a starving man look at a roast dinner in a glass box?

Besides, whatever else it had stirred up, the case had broken the ice. They were given a transfer job next, to take a patient from the emergency department to a convalescent ward in a small rural hospital well north of Wellington. It was over an hour's drive and Kathryn sat in the back with the elderly female patient on the way there. Tim could hear her chatting happily to the woman, who was remarkably fit, considering her age was well into her nineties, and he smiled more than once as he indulged in a spot of shameless eavesdropping. Having a partner who could establish an easy rapport with a patient was a real bonus. There was nothing worse than a long trip with a totally silent set of passengers. The turn of the conversation in the back as they neared their destination made him listen even more carefully.

'So Bill was your *third* husband?'

'They say it's third time lucky, dear, and in my case it was absolutely right.'

'So what happened to your other husbands?'

'The first one ran off with the wife of one of his customers. He sold cars, you know. That was in 1935 and it was a complete scandal. I was far too ashamed to try and get a divorce. It just wasn't done in those days.'

'So how did you manage to marry husband number two?'

'Charlie got himself run over. In his own car yard, would you believe?'

'That was considerate.' Tim could hear the grin in Kathryn's voice.

'I thought so. Mind you, then I married Stanley and he didn't turn out to be a good choice. He hit the bottle rather hard, if you know what I mean. Then he went and got himself killed in the Second World War. It was quite a while before I was tempted to try again but Bill and I had forty wonderful years together. Are you married, dear?'

'Yes.'

'Your first husband?'

Kathryn laughed. 'Yes.'

'How long have you been married?'

'Five years.'

'You look happy enough so I guess you chose the right one.'

'I guess I did.'

Suddenly Tim didn't feel very interested in eavesdropping any further. He turned on the radio and changed stations to find some music that wouldn't offend their patient. Kathryn also seemed inclined to change the subject. Tim could see her on her feet, keeping one hand on a locker handle to keep her balance as she made her patient more comfortable by adjusting her pillow.

'Would you like another blanket, Mrs Ramsey?'

'I'm quite warm enough, thank you, dear. We must be almost there by now, mustn't we?'

'I think so.' Kathryn leaned forward, poking her head into the front compartment. 'How much further is it, Tim?'

'Only another five or ten minutes. It's a nice little hospital. They usually give us a cup of tea before we have to head back.'

Tim insisted on driving back to the city as well. Having something to concentrate on besides his new partner was definitely in order. Keeping the conversation strictly professional also seemed a good idea.

'Any questions you want to ask? About this morning's job?'

'Yes.' Kathryn sounded eager. 'You said the patient was in complete heart block. I'm comfortable with recognising the shockable rhythms but it was a very condensed ECG course and I'm ashamed to say a lot of it went over my head.'

'You can't be expected to know everything. You've got a far better knowledge base than most probationary ambulance officers. You'll find you pick up a lot on the job and you'll have more classroom time coming up as well.'

Tim glanced in Kathryn's direction as he finished speaking, to find her gaze fixed on his face and her eyebrows raised expectantly. She wanted to hear more than reassurance. Tim smiled as he looked ahead at the long, quiet road winding through hills dotted with sheep like mushrooms.

'Complete heart block is third-degree heart block and it's where the atrial contraction is normal but no beats are conducted to the ventricles.'

'So that's why the rate was so slow? It was a ventricular escape rhythm?'

'Yes. And if you look at the trace you'll find p waves that have no relationship to the QRS spikes.'

'We've got a copy of that trace, haven't we?'

'It's rolled up and in with the case report forms.'

Kathryn opened the box compartment of the metal clipboard the forms were attached to. She soon had several metres of trace paper uncurled over her knees, examining the recording that covered the various heart rhythms their case had presented.

'Look, that's where we defibrillated him! Ventricular fibrillation and straight back into sinus rhythm.' Kathryn sighed happily. 'Wasn't it great?'

'Sure was.' Tim enjoyed a moment of the kind of enthusiasm that tended to get blunted by years on this job. His smile was almost one of gratitude for the reminder of what being a paramedic was all about. 'It was *you* that defibrillated him, though.'

Kathryn's nose wrinkled as she grimaced. 'I don't think I could have done it if you hadn't pushed me.'

'It's scary for everybody the first time.'

'I could never do it by myself.'

'Yes, you could, but you'll never need to. We don't work alone. One of our responsibilities is to assess a situation and call for whatever extra assistance we think we're going to need. If you remember, the first thing I did was to call for back-up.'

'I thought that was because you only had me to help.'

'We're a team, Kat. Most of the time we'll be able to handle whatever comes our way all by ourselves.'

Kathryn was staring at him again, but this time her expression wasn't questioning. A play of emotions flitted across her features. Doubt, followed by hope and then a completely charming gratitude that was accompanied by a faint flush of colour in her cheeks. She looked away, clearly embarrassed.

'I hope so,' she said quietly. 'And I can almost believe it with someone like you as a partner.' Her tone advertised a shy determination to say something important. 'You were amazing, Tim. You stay so calm!'

'Just practice.' Tim couldn't remember anyone telling him he was amazing. Ever. 'Besides, you only have to *look* calm. Doesn't matter if you're doing the duck thing and paddling frantically below the surface.'

Kathryn laughed. 'I don't believe you're a duck.'

'That's the best thing about it. Nobody can tell.'

'Yeah. It is amazing what you can hide if you get enough practice, I suppose.'

Tim threw her a quick sideways glance but Kathryn was staring at the trace in her lap again.

'So tell me about the other degrees of heart block, then.'

Tim launched into a mini-lecture that Kathryn seemed only too willing to absorb, but only half his mind was really on the subject. He was doing the duck thing in a way he'd never had to before. Seeming calm and professional on the surface while part of him was paddling frantically and wondering how on earth he could handle working with Kathryn when he found her so incredibly attractive.

It was ironic in a way. Kathryn's intelligence, previous medical experience and obvious passion to excel in her new career made her potentially a perfect partner, on a professional basis as much as anything else. It wasn't her fault that Tim felt irrationally jealous of the man lucky enough to have married her. He knew perfectly well how adolescent such a reaction was and at thirty-five he was old enough and wise enough to know far better.

And even if Kathryn hadn't been married she wouldn't have necessarily returned the interest Tim felt, so maybe it was better this way. He'd never have to face the trauma of offering something that would be rejected. Maybe he should just grow up a little and make the most of what fate had presented him with.

He could enjoy her company, help Kathryn gain the confidence she desperately wanted and undoubtedly deserved, and be grateful for whatever he got offered in return in the way of friendship and professional rapport.

He didn't really have a choice anyway.

Dammit.

Sheer exhaustion was setting in for Kathryn by five o'clock that afternoon. It was a challenge all its own to concentrate on helping Tim restock the ambulance.

'What about the BGL kit?' he queried.

'What about it? Did I do something wrong when I was monitoring that diabetic patient?'

'Not at all. We just need to replace the lancets and test strips we used.'

'Oh, of course. Sorry.'

'Stop apologising, Kat. You're doing fine.'

Kathryn took a deep breath. Had she been saying 'sorry' that often? Maybe she'd been conditioned by Sean. Oddly, she felt compelled to apologise for anything less than perfect for Tim, whereas apologies at home were always grudging these days.

When she came back from the storeroom with all the supplies to tuck into the small case that contained the blood glucose-level testing gear, she found Tim snapping rubber bands around handfuls of differently sized cannulae.

'OK. That's the IV gear done,' he announced. 'Can you think of anything else we've used this afternoon?'

'What about that triangular bandage I used as a sling for that little girl that broke her collar-bone at school?'

'Right. We need more dressings and saline pouches, too. We had that student that got knocked off his bike just after her.'

Kathryn shook her head. 'I'd completely forgotten about him.'

The cases had been so many and varied over the course of the day, they were becoming something of a blur. Except for the very first job. Kathryn would remember that in vivid detail for the rest of her life.

A quick trip to the coronary care unit had been squeezed in after delivering one of their later cases to the emergency department. The satisfaction in finding the man pain-free and virtually unscathed thanks to the angioplasty he had received so promptly to unclog his arteries had carried Kathryn through the rest of the afternoon on a real high. She was only just starting to come down now but the descent seemed to be picking up speed.

Stretching backwards relieved the ache in the small of her back. 'Is it always this busy?'

'No. It's fairly unusual, fortunately.' Tim looked up from checking the gauge on the Entonox cylinder and smiled. 'I'll bet you're stuffed. Why don't you go and put your feet up and have a coffee? I'll finish the truck.'

Kathryn shook her head. 'I'm happy to help.'

'Just do it, Kat.' Tim's smile belied the stern tone and Kathryn grinned as she recognised the echo of the instruction that had pushed her into meeting the challenge their inaugural case together had presented.

She gave Tim a mock salute. 'Yes, *sir*!'

Still smiling, she left the garage and headed for the commonroom. Move over, Nike, she thought. 'Just do it' looked set to become a private joke between her and her new partner.

'You look far too happy to have just finished your first day on the road.'

Startled, Kathryn's head swung towards the archway that separated the dining area of the commonroom from the kitchen.

'I'm Laura,' the young woman told her. 'Tim's old partner?'

'Of course,' Kathryn said. 'I remember you from the restaurant.'

Laura looked blank for a moment, then her jaw dropped. 'You're that nurse!' she exclaimed. 'The one that Tim—' She broke off abruptly and then laughed. 'Did Tim know it was you coming as a probationary officer?'

'I don't think so.' Kathryn was feeling disconcerted now. What had Laura been about to say? And was the uncomfortable start to their day actually because Tim had known she was coming and wasn't pleased about it? A tiny silence fell that neither woman seemed to know how to break. Kathryn took the plunge.

'You're…um, Jason's wife as well?'

'That's right.' Laura's smile was just as pleased as Kathryn's had been on entering the room. 'I'm just making a coffee while I wait for Jase to get back. Would you like one?'

'Please. Black with two sugars.' Kathryn noticed the empty car seat on the floor beside one of the couches. 'Where's your baby?'

'Mrs Mack's taken her for a walk in her new stroller. She'll be back soon.'

'How old is she?' Kathryn accepted the mug of fragrant coffee and sat down with a sigh of relief. Laura sat on the opposite side of the table.

'Who—Mrs Mack or Megan?' Laura laughed. 'Mrs Mack's age is a well-kept secret but I'd say she's in her late sixties. Megan's nearly eleven months old.'

'But you only started your maternity leave this week, didn't you?'

'Yeah. That's because I'm pregnant.' Laura smiled at Kathryn's confusion. 'Long story. Megan is Jason's daughter but it was a bit hard for us both to keep working full time. I decided to take leave and be a full-time mother and we thought if I was at home with one baby, I may as well be at home with two.'

'Sounds like a great idea to me.' Kathryn nodded. She knew she was being assessed, however kindly, by Tim's ex-partner, and she was just as curious herself. Laura was no taller than her own five feet two inches but Kathryn had seen her in action with Tim that night in the restaurant and so she knew just how far ahead she was in the confidence and competence stakes.

'So how's it been? Your first day?'

'Amazing,' Kathryn confessed. 'I defibrillated my first patient on the very first job.'

'Wow! Was it a successful resus?'

'We went to see him in CCU this afternoon. He's going home in a couple of days.'

'Even better.' Laura's gaze was still interested. 'And how are you getting on with Tim?'

'He's great,' Kathryn said enthusiastically. 'I'm going to learn a lot. I just hope he won't get fed up working with me.'

Laura's eyebrows rose. 'I doubt that'll happen in a hurry.' A chuckle escaped, and Kathryn stared.

'Why is that funny?'

'Because you're...um...' Laura glanced towards the door and then lowered her voice. 'Tim was rather taken with you that night in the restaurant. What he failed to notice was the fact that both you and your dinner companion were wearing wedding rings. He was, shall we say, a little disappointed when I pointed out the fact that you were married.'

'Really?' Good grief. Was *that* why Tim hadn't rung? Why things had been so tense this morning? An unexpected flash of regret ambushed Kathryn. What a shame she hadn't met Tim a long time ago. It was far too late now, of course, and she didn't even think of men in those terms any more but suddenly Kathryn could imagine what her reaction to Tim would have been if she *had* still been single. It was enough to bring a flood of colour to her cheeks.

Laura bit her lip. 'I shouldn't have said anything. Tim would *kill* me if he knew. Don't you say anything, will you?'

'I'm hardly likely to.'

'No, I guess not.' Laura still looked worried. 'And you don't have to worry about Tim. He'd never try anything. He knows you're married and that's it as far as he's concerned.'

Kathryn nodded. Of course that was it. As far as either of them were concerned. It did explain a few things, however, and Kathryn felt flattered that she could have inspired any interest in the first place. It had been a long time…no, it might even be the *first* time she had felt really attractive. Attractive enough for somebody to feel disappointed that she wasn't available. Disappointed enough to feel upset even, and to screw up her phone number and throw it in the rubbish.

Laura looked relieved at Kathryn's accepting nod. 'If I've learned one thing about Tim McGrath in the time I worked with him, it's that he's completely honest and totally trustworthy. He's also a great paramedic. There's no way I would have given up working with him if I hadn't had a better offer.' Laura patted her tummy and grinned. 'He's also one of the nicest people I've ever met. You're going to love it here but just remember, you're only keeping *my* seat warm. I'll be back one of these days.'

Tim came into the commonroom as Laura finished talking. 'Yeah, right!' he said. 'You'll be up to your ears in babies for the next few years, Laura Halliday, and you'll be loving every minute of it.'

'Yeah!' Laura grinned at Tim. 'I hear your new partner has been out saving lives.'

'She has indeed.' He looked pointedly at Laura's mug. 'Did you make me a coffee, then?'

'Make it yourself,' Laura retorted. She turned to Kathryn. 'Don't let any of these guys take advantage of the fact you're a woman. They get quite spoilt enough having Mrs Mack around here.'

Tim was heading for the kitchen. 'Speaking of Mackie, I saw her coming down the road with that racy new stroller. She looks as proud as punch.'

'I'll have to drop in more often. She's not going to see nearly as much of Megan now that I'm at home.'

'There's someone else sitting outside the station as well.' Tim spooned coffee into a mug. 'Mackie doesn't have an admirer with a black BMW convertible, by any chance?'

'That'll be the day,' Laura laughed. 'Mackie would scare off any man.'

'It'll be Sean,' Kathryn confessed, her heart sinking. She glanced at the clock. 'It's only five-thirty and he knows I don't finish till six.'

'Ask him in for a coffee.' Tim sat down and reached for a section of the day's newspaper that had been tidied into neat piles at the end of the table.

Kathryn was saved the embarrassment of trying to explain why Sean was unlikely to accept such an invitation by the arrival of the housekeeper, Mrs McKendry, and baby Megan. There was barely time to admire the junior Halliday before her father and the rest of the Green Watch fire crew arrived back on station. New arrivals for the night shift crowded the space, introductions had to be made and suddenly it was six o'clock and time to go home and Kathryn hadn't even made a move to say hello to her waiting husband.

Even then she didn't rush away. She handed her pager over to one of the night crew and followed Tim to collect her bag from her locker. To her acute embarrassment, Sean was waiting for them as they emerged from the locker room.

'It's ten past six, Kathryn. How much longer are you going to be?'

'I'm ready now.' Kathryn put real effort into her smile. 'Sean, this is Tim McGrath. My partner.'

'Tim! Delighted to meet you.' A hand was extended with alacrity and Sean smiled at Kathryn's partner. 'Nice teeth.'

Tim's jaw dropped and Kathryn cringed. 'Sean's a dentist,' she said hurriedly. 'He notices teeth.'

'Oh. In that case, thanks.' Tim cleared his throat self-consciously. 'Can't say I think about them much. I haven't been near a dentist for years.'

'Tch, tch.' Sean extended his hand to take Kathryn's backpack. 'You should see an oral hygienist if nothing else. You might develop receding gums and your teeth will fall out.'

Kathryn stifled a faint groan. She could only hope that Tim wouldn't take this exchange as the kind of put-down it was patently intended to be. Sean clearly wasn't intimidated by having Tim towering over his height of only five feet seven.

'No kidding.' Tim ran his tongue over his front teeth and Kathryn was sure she received another of those ghost winks, like the one sharing her distaste for porridge. 'Know a good hygienist, then, Sean?'

'Come and see Kirsty at my clinic some time. She's the best.'

Kathryn looked pointedly at the door. So Kirsty was 'the best', was she? At least Tim couldn't know that it wouldn't be cleaning teeth that Sean was referring to. How many young hygienists had ended up in her husband's bed over the last five years? It would probably be easier to count the ones who hadn't, but Kathryn had given up counting a long time ago.

Why should she resent the perfect solution? The turnover was high enough to keep Sean happy because he preferred to employ foreigners with limited work permits. Sean was always very discreet and even if Kathryn *did* resent the ongoing situation, she was hardly likely to complain, was she? Sean might be using this opportunity to remind her of her failings but there was no way Kathryn was going to let it ruin her day.

'I've had the most amazing day,' she told Sean brightly as he nodded a farewell to Tim. 'I'll tell you all about it over dinner.'

'We're having dinner at the Gilberts' tonight. I doubt that they will want to be regaled with tales of blood and guts.'

Sean strode ahead towards his car. Kathryn had considered his offer to provide transport a sign that he had finally accepted her new career choice. Now she wasn't so sure. It was humiliating to be picked up like a child attending nursery school.

'I've forgotten my jacket,' she exclaimed. 'I left it in the truck.'

'Can't it wait until tomorrow?'

'No, it might get lost. Sorry, Sean, I'll only be a second.'

She ran through the side door of the garage and promptly collided with Tim.

'Whoa!' he said, holding her arm to steady her. 'It can't be that urgent.'

'Sorry. I forgot my jacket.'

'I know. Stop apologising. I was just bringing it out for you.' Tim had the garment draped over his arm.

'Thanks.' Kathryn took the jacket and then hesitated. 'I'd better get going. Sean hates being late.'

'See you tomorrow, then.'

Still Kathryn hesitated. 'I just wanted to say thanks, Tim.' She met his gaze and smiled. 'It's been a wicked day.'

'We'll have another one tomorrow.'

'OK.' Kathryn's smile widened. 'And I'll try not to say "sorry" so often.'

'I'm not sure I said it often enough myself. I *am* sorry I never rang you to tell you about that patient, you know. I hope you don't think I break all my promises.'

'It really doesn't matter,' Kathryn told him. 'See you in the morning.'

Running outside again, Kathryn made a beeline for the black BMW. Apart from being delivered and collected and the subtle sniping Sean had indulged in, the day had been as close to perfect as she could have hoped. Even the tension of her meeting with Tim this morning had just become insignificant.

It really *didn't* matter.

Not any more.

CHAPTER THREE

AS SABOTAGE went, it was subtle but very effective.

A glance at her elegant gold wristwatch told Kathryn it was nearly 11 p.m. She would have to be up at 6 a.m. to get to work on time and she was already so tired that large chunks of the dinner-table conversation kept turning into an incomprehensible buzz.

It was torture. Kathryn pushed her spoon into the overly rich chocolate dessert she knew she couldn't eat and then looked up, hoping that the movement would make it easier to keep her eyes open. She was sitting directly opposite her husband, it was inevitable that their lines of vision would meet. When had Kathryn ever looked up to find Sean looking somewhere else?

'You look tired, darling.'

The tone was caring but the hint of triumph in the green eyes was enough to make her blink and then force a bright smile. The sabotage was not going to succeed. She would not give Sean the ammunition of breaking her promise that her new career would not be allowed to interfere with their social life.

'Do I?' Kathryn managed to sound faintly surprised. She kept smiling but there was genuine amusement in her expression now. Even if her exhaustion had aged her twenty years she would still look young in this gathering. It was hard to believe that being drawn into such circles had once made her feel privileged. And special. The looks she could feel coming in her direction at the moment, as conversation around the table petered out, branded her the misfit they had all suspected she really was. Not that Sean picked up any undercurrents.

'Kathryn started a new job today,' he announced in the short silence. 'She's become an ambulance driver.'

'A paramedic, actually.' Kathryn couldn't stop herself making the correction but hopefully she kept her tone light enough to avoid creating any ammunition for Sean to use later. 'We do quite a lot more than just driving the ambulances.'

'Oh, my goodness!' Evelyn Gilbert touched the rope of pearls at her neck.

Dorothy Harrison looked equally appalled. 'How could you do that, Kathryn? All those *dreadful* car accidents!'

Kathryn could feel the satisfaction coming at her from across the table. 'Blood and guts' was most definitely an inappropriate topic.

'Car accidents are actually a very small percentage of the workload,' she said quietly. 'Most of our emergency cases are medical. Things like asthma or diabetes or heart attacks.' She smiled at the other husbands around the gleaming mahogany table.

At forty-five, Sean was by far the youngest of this group. Some of them were pushing sixty and they all looked prosperous and very well fed.

'My first job today was a heart-attack victim, in fact. A fifty-six-year-old man who'd never had a day off work sick in his life.' Kathryn glanced down at her dessert with distaste. Surely these people could see that the kind of lifestyle they led made them all potential candidates for a nasty cardiac event?

Donald Harrison was looking rather thoughtfully at his empty parfait glass. 'Was he all right?'

'He was dreadfully ill,' Kathryn said with satisfaction. 'And then he arrested.'

'You mean he *died*?' Evelyn, the hostess for this evening, went a shade paler and cast an anxious glance at her other guests.

'No. He's fine now. I defibrillated him.' Kathryn couldn't help the note of pride in her voice. 'We got him into hospital fast and he had an angioplasty within a couple of hours of the onset of his chest pain. He'll be going home in a day or two.'

Donald smiled with obvious relief. 'Well done,' he congratulated Kathryn. 'That must have been rather satisfying.'

'It was wicked,' Kathryn agreed. She ignored the frown on Sean's face that was intended as a reminder of how much he disapproved of slang.

'I had to call an ambulance once.' Dorothy's husband Donald was nodding. 'Had a chap who had a rather unpleasant reaction to the IV sedation I gave him.'

'That's why I never use the stuff,' Sean declared. 'A good local should always do the job. I use gas if I have to, but you all know my views on that.'

The common topic of dentistry had been well aired over the main course. Donald drained his glass of red wine and stared at Kathryn as though she were a new and interesting exhibit at the art gallery.

'A paramedic, hmm?' He turned to Sean. 'I'm amazed you're letting your wife run around on the streets doing a dangerous job like that, old chap.' His gaze returned to Kathryn, making her wish she hadn't gone the extra mile to keep Sean happy that evening by wearing this particular black dress. It was cut rather too low for her comfort. 'Don't you have to work nights as well?'

This wasn't a safe topic. 'Yes, but the hours are great, really,' she said lightly. 'We work four days on, including two nights, and then have four days off. It's almost a part-time job, in fact. Not that different from what I was doing with Dr Braithwaite.' Kathryn smiled again. 'It's only two days and two nights out of eight, which means I'm home for six days and six nights out of eight. Sean will probably not even notice.'

'Not true,' Sean protested. Only Kathryn heard the warning note.

'How *is* dear old Angus Braithwaite?' Evelyn latched onto a new conversational direction with alacrity. 'I haven't seen him *or* Mary for such a long time.'

'He never changes,' Sean told her. 'I did some reconstruction work for him a month or two back. He claimed it made him look ten years younger.'

'Wonderful man,' Dorothy cooed. She smiled at Kathryn. 'He was telling me about your mother the last time we met. How *is* she these days?'

Kathryn tried to return the smile but failed miserably. 'She's very well looked after.'

'There's not much you can do for advanced multiple sclerosis other than keep the sufferer comfortable,' Sean added.

'I've heard that Hillsborough is *the* place as far as nursing homes go.' Donald refilled his wineglass. 'Might make a reservation for myself one of these years. Lap-of-luxury stuff, isn't it?' He raised the bottle. 'A top-up, Sean?'

'Just a half, thanks. I'm driving.' Sean held out his glass. 'You'll need to save your pennies for Hillsborough, Don. A minimum of a thousand dollars a week isn't cheap.'

'Good heavens.' Evelyn Gilbert looked impressed. 'That's twice as much as the place my father's in.'

'You get what you pay for,' Sean said lightly. 'And nothing's too good for my mother-in-law.' He had to balance his glass carefully as the liquid touched the rim. 'That's a generous half there, Don.'

'You're a generous man,' his colleague responded. 'Not many people would care for their mother-in-law like that.

I'm sure you don't get *that* much of a discount for being a shareholder in the place.'

'I don't take any discount.'

More than one glance told Kathryn how lucky she was, and this time Kathryn managed to smile back. This kind of approbation would make Sean happy and the happier Sean Mercer was, the more tolerable her life became. He'd be on top of the world not to have had to engineer such a blatant reminder of why she would be unwise to ever raise the topic of a divorce again.

'It's almost as bad as having three children in private schools.' Dennis Gilbert made one of his rare contributions to the conversation at one of his wife's dinner parties. 'Thank goodness we're on the countdown to getting the last one off our hands.'

'You haven't even started on that caper, Sean.' Donald's smile was knowing. 'You'll have to step up that chair-side porcelain work to keep the bank manager happy.'

'We'll manage.' Sean's smile was appearing frequently enough to ease Kathryn's familiar tension. 'Cosmetic dentistry is booming.'

'So you *are* planning to have children?' Dorothy Harrison couldn't help herself. 'That's wonderful, Sean.'

'About time,' Donald concurred. 'You don't want to be booking into Hillsborough by the time they get to university.'

'Kathryn's promised it'll only take a year to get this new craze out of her system. Then it'll be ''bye-bye paramedic'' and ''hello parenthood''.'

Kathryn's smile felt pasted into place. Of course she had made that promise. She would have made whatever promises it took, and that had been the one that had finally persuaded Sean not to make her new career an impossibility. Sheer desperation had pushed her to actually agree to undergo IVF and produce a child so that Sean would have visible evidence that success in his private life matched his considerable professional achievements.

A lot could happen in a year, though, couldn't it? He might even get used to her working shifts. Kathryn tried, and failed, to quell the seed of hope that had taken root over the last few months of her training. A year could give her the time and a new career could give her the base to find a way out.

Out of her promises.

Possibly even out of her sham of a marriage.

Happily, Sean had no hint of the direction of Kathryn's thoughts. He finished his wine before using a starched linen napkin to blot his lips. 'This has been a most pleasant evening but we'd better make a move, Evelyn. Kathryn has to get up at the crack of dawn to pursue her new career and I suspect she's falling asleep on us already.'

'Oh, but you haven't eaten your dessert, Kathryn!'

Sean was ready to make excuses on her behalf. 'I've eaten enough for both of us. It was absolutely delicious.' He pulled Kathryn's chair back. 'And when you're vertically challenged you *do* need to watch that the pounds don't pile on.'

Everyone except Kathryn laughed politely, but the party was over and the Mercers weren't the only guests to head out into the chilly night.

'We're not through the worst of winter yet. Feels like there's going to be a frost tonight.'

'Just think of Madrid,' Donald reminded his wife. 'It's not that long till October and we'll have some autumn in Spain instead of the usual rubbish that spring throws at us in Wellington.'

'I can't wait,' Dorothy enthused. 'We'll have such fun in the shops, won't we, Kathryn?'

'Kathryn won't be going to Spain.'

'What? But you're a keynote speaker at the conference, Sean.'

'I'm on a six-month probationary period with the ambulance service. I couldn't take time off halfway through.'

Meaningful glances were exchanged around her and Kathryn sighed inwardly. The good humour engendered by the dinner party had just been negated by the reminder of yet another point she and Sean had argued about. Climbing into the sleek BMW convertible, Kathryn tilted her head back and closed her eyes. Only six hours to go and she would be heading back to the only place she wanted to be. It didn't matter that she felt too tired to think straight. She'd cope.

She had always been able to cope.

It was patently obvious that someone wasn't coping.

Kathryn heard the muffled sound of sobbing coming from the back of the ambulance parked beside her own vehicle as she came out of the emergency department. One of the back doors was slightly ajar, as though someone had tried to close it but hadn't latched it properly. Kathryn paused, creating a tug on the end of the stretcher being pulled by Tim.

She tilted her head towards the sound. 'Is it a patient, do you think?'

Tim's face creased into the lines of concern that Kathryn could recognise so easily now. She knew that the concern would be genuine and that Tim would not share her own reluctance to intrude. When he pulled the door open far enough for her to see the young ambulance officer hunched on the stretcher in the back of the ambulance, Kathryn's hesitation also vanished.

'Jo—whatever's the matter?' In a second, Kathryn was sitting beside the woman with her arm around the heaving shoulders.

'I can't do this job,' Jo sobbed. 'I hate it.'

Kathryn looked up as Tim climbed into the ambulance and pulled the doors closed behind him. 'This is Jo, Tim. She was in my class.' Her hold tightened on her colleague. 'It's only been a few shifts, Jo. Is it really that bad?'

'Yes!'

'You're working with Bruce Stanton, aren't you?' Jo nodded as Tim pressed a wad of tissues into her hands. He sat down on the opposite stretcher, still holding the tissue box. 'And you just had an unsuccessful arrest case?'

'You heard him, didn't you?' Jo blew her nose vigorously but her tears hadn't stopped. 'Telling that doctor how useless I am? Saying how he expected a few more trips to the morgue if he had to keep working with someone like me?'

'What a jerk,' Kathryn said indignantly. 'As if it was your fault!'

'But I did everything wrong,' Jo said with a fresh sob. 'Bruce expects me to know what to do and then he gets angry when I'm not fast enough and I get flustered and make some *stupid* mistake. Like putting the leads on wrong, like I did this time.'

Kathryn caught Tim's gaze and a corner of her partner's mouth quirked ever so slightly. They could both remember the day Kathryn had made precisely the same error. She had stared in consternation at the peculiar rhythm on the screen and Tim had said, very mildly, 'You might like to swap the left arm and leg leads over when you've a second, Kat.'

His tone was just as mild now. 'Bruce isn't known for his tolerance, Jo. Don't let him put you down.'

'I know he's got problems at home.' Jo sniffed and then

blew her nose again. 'But he shouldn't be taking them out on me, should he?'

'Of course he shouldn't,' Kathryn said fervently.

'And if he treats his wife like he treats me, I'm not surprised she's walked out on him.'

Tim was frowning now. 'There's no excuse for letting personal problems affect a professional relationship. Have you spoken to any of the training managers about it?'

Jo shook her head. 'I don't want to make things any worse.'

Kathryn closed her eyes for a second. It would be easy to tell Jo that that wouldn't work in the long run, but who was she kidding? It was precisely the reasoning she had used at home for the last five years.

'I thought it would get better,' Jo continued sadly. 'But it's been nearly a month and it's only getting worse. I'm going to resign.'

'Oh, no, don't do that.' Kathryn bit her lip. Jo must be feeling terrible. Kathryn couldn't even imagine wanting to resign. Every shift she did was better than the last, and already her periods of four days off were simply marking time before she could get back to work.

Even the physical exhaustion of her new career was receding. Kathryn felt strong enough to handle anything as long as she had Tim standing in the wings, if not leading directly. Jo's predicament showed her just how different things could have been, and Kathryn felt a wave of gratitude that must have showed in her smile because Tim looked embarrassed.

'I'm going to go and have a quiet word with Bruce,' he said.

'No—you'll just make it worse!'

Tim reached forward and rubbed his thumb on Jo's cheek. 'No, I won't,' he said gently. 'Promise!'

'It'll get better.' Kathryn tried to reassure her classmate after Tim had gone. 'Bruce just needs to get to know you better.'

'Ha!' Jo sniffed again but Kathryn was pleased to see that she had stopped crying. 'You get to know someone remarkably fast shut up in a truck with them day and night for weeks. He hates me. And I'm scared of him.'

'It's no wonder you're making mistakes, working in an atmosphere like that. Maybe Tim's right and you should talk to someone about it.'

'I feel better now. Maybe Bruce will listen to Tim.' A watery smile appeared on Jo's face. 'He's lovely, isn't he? You're so lucky, Kat.'

'I know. Tim's brilliant. You should see the way he interacts with patients. Everybody loves him.'

'Is he married?' Jo was perking up quickly now. 'Or with someone?'

'No. At least I don't *think* so.' Kathryn had been so careful not to reveal too much of her own personal life that she hadn't realised how little she really knew about Tim's. A flash of curiosity surfaced that clearly equalled Jo's. 'I'll find out, shall I?'

'Yes, please.' Jo's smile was a lot brighter. 'You could give him my phone number if you like.'

'OK.' Kathryn stood up. Through the back window of the ambulance, she could see Tim and Bruce as they came out of the emergency department. 'Can't guarantee he'll ring, though. I hear he's bad with phone numbers.'

'Doesn't matter. I'm bound to run into him again around here.'

'Not if you resign, you won't.'

'I'd better stick it out for a while longer, then, hadn't I?'

Kathryn stepped down from the ambulance. She could

hear Bruce behind her as she caught up with Tim's long stride.

'Sorry, Jo. Guess I've been a bit hard on you, haven't I?'

'Jo wants me to give you her phone number.'

'Why?'

Kathryn gave Tim an old-fashioned look. 'Why do you think?'

'Oh...' Tim seemed to be concentrating hard on the red traffic light. 'I wouldn't bother. I'm bad with phone numbers.'

The tiny silence wasn't uncomfortable. Kathryn and Tim might not be well versed in each other's private lives but an understanding had been reached on that particular matter on their first day together. Jo had been right in her opinion of how quickly and how well you got to know the people you worked with on a job like this, and the more time Kathryn spent with her partner, the more she trusted and liked him.

'That was a nice thing to do, intervening with Bruce. I hope it helps.'

'I'm sure it will. I doubt that Bruce had any idea he was making things so awful for Jo. He's just got a lot going on at the moment.'

'So I gathered.'

'Not just at home.' Tim pulled away as the light changed to green. 'Bruce is a bit frustrated. He'd rather be on the helicopters than the road. He's addicted to the adrenalin rush, I think. Even his hobbies have to have an edge. He broke his leg paragliding last year.'

'Being out on the road is quite exciting enough for me.'

'And me.' Tim nodded. 'But, then, I'm considered boring.'

'Who by?' Kathryn asked indignantly.

'Anyone who spends time with me outside working hours, I guess.' Tim gave Kathryn a quick grin. 'So there's another reason why you shouldn't bother giving me Jo's phone number.' He snorted softly as he slowed for another set of lights. 'Even Laura told me I was "safe". That's pretty close to boring.'

'No, it's not.' Kathryn could agree with the impression of safety. She was clocking up more and more instances where she had relied completely on that solid dependability. And working with Tim was in no way boring. 'They're nothing like the same thing.'

'But if something's boring then it's got to be safe. If it's dangerous then it's definitely not boring.'

Kathryn shook her head. 'Some of the best things in the world are safe and they're certainly not boring.'

'Such as?'

'Reading a book,' Kathryn responded promptly. A shopping centre was slipping past as they headed back to the station, but she wasn't looking at the scenery. She had, in fact, closed her eyes. 'Lying on a hilltop, counting stars. Walking on a deserted beach.' Her tone became unconsciously wistful. 'Spending time with someone that you love.'

'Safe' was a word that conjured up distant memories. These days, it had all the allure of the unattainable.

Tim's voice sounded oddly strained. 'Do you do that sort of thing often, then?'

Kathryn's eyes snapped open. What on earth had made her say something like *that*? She had to be very tired to let her guard down that much. A glance at her watch told her they still had half a night shift to spend together. Backing off was definitely in order.

'Yeah. I read a *lot*,' she said lightly.

'How 'bout counting stars?'

'The last time I did that I was about ten years old. My

dad knew the names of every star I asked about. At least, he *told* me a name for every star.'

Kathryn shook her head imperceptibly as she pushed the poignant memory back where it belonged. Her guard must really be weak for some reason, she decided. Maybe it was because Jo had made her aware of how lucky she was in the mentor she had been assigned. That feeling of gratitude was still with her. Or maybe it was the sparking of her curiosity regarding Tim's private life. Jo wasn't about to find out much, was she? Kathryn knew she had no reason at all to feel pleased that Tim wasn't interested in calling her classmate, but the reaction was undeniable, nonetheless.

'What about you?' she found herself asking.

'I've never counted stars,' he said. 'See—told you I was boring.'

'What *do* you do on your days off?'

'Renovate.' Tim laughed when he caught Kathryn's expectant expression. 'That's it, or at least that's how it feels. I started work on my house about two years ago and there's no sign of finishing it any time soon.'

'Must be a very big house.'

'No. It's just very, very old and my parents never bothered stripping back the woodwork. They'd just add another layer of paint every few years.'

'You live with your parents?' Kathryn tried to sound casual but the thought of a thirty-something male still living at home might actually give some support to a 'boring' label.

'Are you kidding?' Tim's glance was speculative enough to cause embarrassment at even thinking such a thing. 'My parents died ten years ago. I inherited the house and orchard and, seeing it's been in the family for four generations, I thought I'd better try and keep it going on my days off. Keeps me busy, anyway.'

'What sort of orchard is it?'

'Apple.'

Kathryn laughed. 'What sort of apples?'

'All sorts. Granny Smiths, Braeburns, Gala, Cox's Orange. You're not really interested in *apples*, are you?'

'I like eating them. Where is your orchard?'

'Way up the Hutt Valley. The house was built in 1870. It's the oldest in the district.'

'My dad spent a lot of time doing up the old villa I grew up in. I love old houses.'

'Come and see mine some time. Be warned, though, you'll probably end up with a paint scraper in your hand. I've just started the banisters and it's a six-month job at least.' Tim grinned at her. 'And it's boring as hell.'

'Sounds fun to me.' Kathryn didn't want Tim to think of himself as boring. He *wasn't*. Not by a very long shot. He was kind and caring and often very funny. No wonder Jo had been so instantly attracted. Once again Kathryn had the weird sensation of feeling pleased that Tim wasn't returning that interest. 'Modern houses are boring,' she added quickly, to distract herself. 'They've got no real character. Sean's house is all clean and white and there wouldn't be any point in trying to scrape wrought-iron banisters.'

'Sean's house?'

Kathryn could feel her cheeks heating at such an obvious slip. What was wrong with her tonight? 'Our house,' she amended. 'I've just always thought of it as Sean's because he was living in it before we got married.'

The pagers sounding filled the silence that followed Kathryn's hasty explanation. She pushed the buttons, taking rather longer to decipher the message than normal due to the relief at the forced change of conversational subject.

Not that Tim ever followed up any opportunities for asking personal questions. Laura had been telling the truth when she'd said that any interest Tim may have had in her had been dismissed the moment he'd learned she was married. Their relationship was as strictly professional as was possible given the type of job they did and the hours spent exclusively in each other's company.

Jo had been right as well. It was astonishing how well you could get to know somebody in this profession in such a short space of time. Whole days from 7 a.m. to 6 p.m. Whole nights from 6 p.m. till 7 a.m. Busy times sharing challenges or just coping with job after job. Quiet times of sitting on station or longer drives to rural areas when conversation unrelated to work was a way of stress relief or simply recharging personal batteries.

'Got all that?' Tim interrupted the direction of Kathryn's thoughts. 'You don't need to look up the address. I know that street.'

'What's the bit about the key on the pager for?'

'Must be a safe house alarm.' Tim activated the beacons and did a U-turn. 'We'll get a call in a minute to tell us where the key is hidden.'

Kathryn answered the radio message. 'No response to a phone call,' they were informed. 'The key is under the third gnome from the right, between the two blue flowerpots.' The voice from the control room sounded amused. 'Apparently the gnome has a green hat. Have fun!'

The job wasn't far away and the row of garden gnomes easy enough to find, but there was no key under the one with the green hat.

'There's no key under any of these gnomes,' Kathryn concluded. 'What do we do now?'

'Let's try the door.' Tim put down the last flowerpot he had checked. 'It's probably nothing anyway. A lot of these personal alarms are activated when someone rolls over in bed. If they've taken their hearing aids out for the night, they don't hear the phone call to check on them so we have to be despatched.'

'It must scare old people to have someone creeping into their house in the middle of the night when they're sound asleep.'

'You're not wrong.' Tim looked positively mischievous. 'I reckon we're going to give someone a heart attack and kill them one of these days.'

Kathryn tried the doorhandle. 'It's locked,' she reported. She knocked on the door softly. 'I can hear something,' she said. She knocked more loudly. 'Hello? Ambulance here. Can you hear me?'

'Hello-o-o.' The voice was faint and quavery. 'Who's there?'

'Ambulance,' Tim said loudly. He winked at Kathryn. 'Can you come and open the door for us?'

'No-o-o.'

'Why not?'

'I can't get up.'

'Are you injured?'

After a long silence, what sounded remarkably like a giggle floated through the thick wood of the front door. 'I don't know. Who did you say you were?'

Tim sighed. 'There's no key under the gnome,' he shouted. 'Is there a door or window open anywhere so we can get in and check on you?'

There was no answer. Tim called again and they waited. They knocked again and waited some more. A minute stretched into two and then three, still with no response from inside the house.

Tim stepped back and shone his torch on the windows. 'They all look pretty secure. Let's check around the back.'

Feeling like a burglar, Kathryn followed Tim into an unkempt rear section, trying each window as they went and shining their torches into the dark house.

'She must be lying on the floor in the front hall,' Kathryn decided aloud. 'Do you think she *is* injured? Bit odd, the way she just stopped talking like that.'

'We won't know until we get in. We'll have to break a window.'

They were standing beside the back door now and the glass panel looked like the obvious choice. 'We'll just have to hope there's a key on the other side,' Tim said.

'What about the louvre window?' Kathryn pointed upwards. 'It must be a toilet or something in there.'

'The louvres are easy enough to get out,' Tim agreed, 'but that's a mighty small window and, in case you hadn't noticed, I'm not a very small man.'

'No.' Kathryn eyed Tim's solid body. 'But I am.'

'A small man?' Tim grinned. 'I don't think so.'

The reminder of what Tim had once thought of her as a woman was disconcerting. 'I'm small enough to get through the window,' she declared. 'Just watch.' Kathryn dragged a rubbish bin closer to the wall and climbed on top of it. 'I'll pass the glass down to you,' she told Tim. 'This should be nice and quick.'

Getting the glass panels out was quick enough. Getting Kathryn through the window turned into a problem. Tim provided the extra height needed by letting Kathryn use his shoulder as a step but having got the front half of her body through the tiny window she found herself stuck. She could feel her legs dangling down the outside wall of the house and she could see a toilet rather a long way below her.

'Hello-o.' The quavery voice sounded a lot louder from inside the house. 'Who's there?'

The ridiculousness of her situation struck Kathryn and, instead of trying to wriggle herself into a sideways position so she could get further forward, she found herself incapacitated by giggles.

'Are you all right?' The muffled query came from outside.

'Hello-o,' came from inside.

'I'm stuck,' Kathryn squeaked eventually.

'What?'

'I'm *stuck*!' Kathryn yelled.

'Who's there?' The old lady sounded distinctly frightened now. 'Go away!'

Then Kathryn felt some large, firm hands on her bottom and suddenly she didn't feel like giggling any more.

'I'll give you a bit of a shove,' Tim was saying.

Kathryn couldn't say anything. Tim had touched her before in the line of duty, like the time he'd showed her a better way of holding the IV cannula when searching for a vein, or when she had stumbled while negotiating a rough path in the dark, but it had never felt like this. The heat she could feel in her face couldn't be simply attributed to the fact she was hanging head down. The odd cramping in her gut had nothing to do with fear of falling head first into the toilet either.

Odd things were happening tonight and they added up to a realisation Kathryn had been doing her best to avoid. It didn't matter that she wasn't single. She was attracted to Tim McGrath more than she had ever been attracted to any man. And right now the sensations she was experiencing had absolutely nothing to do with any of the commendable personality traits her partner exhibited. This was lust, pure and simple.

Her hips slid another inch or two through the narrow frame and Kathryn was able to twist, holding the frame with one hand while hooking one leg clear. She looked down at Tim.

'Thanks…I think.'

'You're welcome.' Tim was grinning broadly. 'In fact, it was something of a pleasure. Can you get down now?'

'Sure. If you hear a scream, it'll be because I've fallen into the loo.'

Kathryn managed to reach the floor safely and she breathed a sigh of relief on finding a light switch. It took only a matter of seconds to unlock the back door and then a far more professional atmosphere returned.

But not for long. The old lady lying on the floor of her front hallway was quite obviously drunk.

'Hello-o,' she greeted the ambulance crew. 'I can't get up.'

'What's your name?'

'Enid. What's yours?'

'I'm Kathryn and this is Tim. Does anything hurt, Enid?'

'No. I'm fine, thank you, dear.'

Kathryn wrinkled her nose at Tim who had moved behind the woman's head. He mimed drinking from a glass and then stood there with a huge and unhelpful grin on his face.

'Ah…have you been drinking tonight, Enid?'

'Never touch the stuff, dear.'

'How did you fall over?'

'It was Harry. He tripped me up, the little rascal.'

'Is Harry your cat?'

'No. You probably met him on your way in. He's out in the garden with his friends again now. The one with the green hat. Very sneaky is Harry.'

Kathryn had to press a hand to her mouth and disguise a wild giggle by coughing. Tim wiped the grin off his face and his voice was that of a caring professional.

'What say we get you up off this floor, Enid? Then you can go to the loo and we'll make sure you're tucked up safely in bed before we go.'

* * *

Kathryn was still dissolving into periodic bursts of giggles as they drove back to the station some time later.

'Enid's son wasn't very happy about being woken up, was he?'

'He was muttering fairly darkly about it being time his mother went into care, that's for sure.'

'Does he know she's an alcoholic?'

'He does now.' Tim shook his head. 'She's obviously kept it very well hidden for a long time. I was beginning to wonder myself when we couldn't find any evidence other than the smell of her breath.'

'It's useful to be clumsy occasionally,' Kathryn grinned. 'If I hadn't kicked one of those chocolate boxes in her bedroom, I'd never have thought of opening them to look for bottles.'

'How many were there?'

'Dozens. Her son always gives her chocolates. He thought she just liked collecting the boxes.'

'And gnomes. Don't forget the gnomes.'

'Don't! It's starting to hurt to laugh.' Kathryn clutched her sides as another giggle escaped. It was just as well she wasn't driving. It was her turn to drive but Tim had got into the habit of insisting on doing most of the driving at night. He said he was used to shift work and Kathryn still got tired enough to make driving an unnecessary extra.

Tim was looking thoughtful as he slowed for a sharp corner. 'Seems to me like you don't use your funny muscles nearly often enough in that case. We'll have to do something about that.'

Kathryn's sigh was happy. 'I never knew this job could be so much fun. We get some really crazy calls sometimes, don't we?'

'Especially on a full moon,' Tim agreed. 'People like Enid certainly add entertainment value, but they can be frustrating if we're being held up when we're needed somewhere genuine in a hurry.'

'Hmm.' Kathryn hadn't considered the wider implications. Amusement faded and she sighed far less happily. 'I hope Jo's going to be OK. It would be a real shame if she resigned. She was one of the best in our class.'

'I'll follow it up,' Tim said. 'If things don't improve, they'll have to find her a new mentor. If it's a personality clash, that could be all that's needed. Trouble is, there's not that many of us available. She might have to swap with someone.'

'Don't look at me!' Kathryn's eyes widened in alarm. 'You don't *want* to swap me, do you?'

'Hell, no.' Tim missed the change of traffic light from red to green because he was looking at Kathryn, but it didn't matter. The suburban streets in this area were totally deserted at 2 a.m. 'I'm way too selfish. I reckon I got the pick of the bunch.'

Kathryn shook her head. 'Doubt it. What about that first IV I did this evening? Took me three goes.'

'Not your fault it was a ninety-something-year-old who was dehydrated enough to make veins hard to find and then they're as fragile as hell when you do find them. Might have taken me *six* goes.'

'Doubt it,' Kathryn said again with even more conviction. 'And I should have got an 18 gauge in. A 20 was too small for the fluid replacement she needed. She'd been lying on the floor with that fractured hip for two days.'

'Better to get a 20 in than nothing. We still got a litre of fluid on board by the time we got to Emergency.'

Kathryn grinned. 'Only because you drove so slowly.'

'Well, you needed time to do the paperwork.' They were moving again now, but Tim took a hand off the wheel to rub the back of his neck as he stretched. 'Only five hours to go and then four days off. Cool, huh?'

Kathryn wished she could do more than nod. She couldn't look forward to her days off when it felt like she was finishing a temporary release from prison. At least she still had five hours of reprieve left.

'I'll try and catch up with Jo in the next day or two,' she told Tim, 'and give her some encouragement. She'd really regret it if she *did* resign.'

'Not everybody loves this job as much as you seem to, Kat.'

'I've been lucky,' Kathryn said seriously. 'I reckon I got the pick of the bunch as far as mentors went.'

Tim shrugged off the compliment. 'At least I've never made you cry.'

'I never cry.'

'Really?' Tim's sideways glance was curious. 'What… never?'

'Nah. Gave it up years ago.' She'd *used* it up years ago, anyway. A whole lifetime's supply of tears gone in the first year of her marriage. 'Ruins your mascara,' she added with a grin. 'Or hadn't you noticed?'

'Can't say I had.' Tim glanced at her again. 'You're tough, aren't you? You wouldn't think so to look at you, but I reckon you could cope with just about anything.'

'With you pushing me, I probably can,' Kathryn conceded. 'I would never have attempted straightening that compound fracture the other day if you hadn't given me that look.'

'What look?'

'The "just do it, Kat" look.'

Tim chuckled. 'Well, it had to be done. She'd lost her radial pulse and sensation in her fingers. Nerve damage to a hand is something that really needs to be avoided if possible. Besides, she had plenty of morphine on board.'

'It still hurt. And it was so gross, seeing the bone sucked back into her arm like that.'

'Felt good finding a pulse again, though, didn't it?'

'Yeah.' Kathryn smiled.

'And you won't be nearly as freaked out the next time you have to do it.'

'Not if you're there, glaring at me.'

'I never glare.'

'No.' Kathryn's agreement was soft. 'You're brilliant, Tim. Talking to Jo tonight made me realise just how lucky I am. I've never said thank you properly, have I?'

'You've stopped saying sorry all the time. That'll do me.' Tim braked as they waited for the automatic garage doors of Inglewood station to roll up. 'The downside of a job like this can be the amount of time you spend with your crew partner,' he observed. 'It's still quite possible to function well if you don't get on, but it takes an awful lot of pleasure away from the job.'

The garage doors were open now but the ambulance wasn't moving. 'It's a real bonus if you work with someone you really like,' Tim concluded.

His smile was fleeting and the faint embarrassment it contained let Kathryn know that he was talking in very personal terms here.

A whirl of thoughts took only a split second for her brain to process.

It couldn't hurt to let Tim know how much *she* liked *him*, could it? It didn't have to reveal anything more than a professional compatibility, did it? And she *did* like Tim, quite apart from the physical attraction she was now so aware of.

So Kathryn returned the smile. She even held the gaze

from those warm brown eyes a fraction longer than felt acceptable in professional terms. And why not?

She *did* like Tim McGrath…as a person and not just as a paramedic.

She liked him a *lot*.

CHAPTER FOUR

EMERGENCY vehicle beacons lit up the night sky.

From far enough above the scene, the strobe effect of red, blue and white might have looked as though a huge party was in progress. At ground level, it was clear it was anything but a celebration.

The entire crew of Inglewood station, both fire and ambulance, arrived shortly after police had secured the accident scene, blocking any movement of both north- and southbound traffic on the motorway. Fortunately, the time of 2 a.m. meant any traffic build-up was not going to be much of a problem. The emergency personnel had quite enough to deal with.

'What the hell's happened here?' Kathryn could hear Jason Halliday's query directed at a police officer as she climbed out of the back of the ambulance, carrying a resuscitation kit and a portable oxygen cylinder.

'That red Nissan's come around that bend, crossed the centre line and collected the white Holden.'

Kathryn stared at the scene. It looked like more than two vehicles had been involved.

'The Nissan's sheared in half. That's the front end of it on the other side of the road.'

A scatter of debris, including large chunks of metal, glass and puddles of what looked like oil, marked the path the car's engine compartment had taken. The remaining section of the red vehicle was now clearly empty and resting about five metres from the white Holden.

Kathryn couldn't see into the second one. The front was

crushed, the bonnet buckled and raised and the windscreen had shattered but was not displaced. The car was tipped to one side and the backs of the heavy protective jackets with reflective strips being worn by both fire and police officers were blocking any view into the side windows.

The impression of how serious a crash this was took only a second or two and then Tim was standing beside her. The nearby police officer turned as he heard Tim speaking.

'What have we got?' The query was brisk.

'Driver of the Nissan appears OK,' they were informed. 'The airbag deployed and he walked away from the wreck. I'd say his blood alcohol level is well over the limit.'

They were all moving towards the second vehicle now.

'Two people in the Holden,' the police officer continued. 'Both look pretty seriously injured. The driver was unconscious when we arrived but he's come around. We can't get near him. There's access to the female passenger through the window but the door's jammed.'

Bruce and Cliff were already assessing the wreck.

'We've got fuel leaking,' Kathryn heard someone shout.

'Let's get some foam onto it, then.'

'Car's not stable,' Bruce warned Tim. 'We'll get some chocks into place now. Don't lean on anything yet.'

'OK.' Tim's access to the passenger door was blocked by Jason. He tapped the fireman on his shoulder. 'How 'bout some space, mate?'

'Sorry.' Jason stepped back. 'Her name's Wendy,' he told Tim. He stepped further back to let Kathryn closer. 'She's not looking too good. And we're going to have to cut that door away to give you any real access.'

'Grab a large dressing, Kat,' Tim ordered. 'Can you bring that light back here again, please, Jase?'

They crowded round the tiny patch of access the side window afforded and Kathryn had to stifle a gasp at her first view of the injured passenger. She must have hit her head on the dashboard. She had a huge laceration from one side of her mouth up past her nose and another towards her ear. Yet another had lifted the scalp from one side of her forehead and peeled it halfway back over her head. Copious amounts of blood were streaming down her face and the woman was sobbing hysterically.

'Get me out… Get me *out*! John! *John!* Are you still here?'

'It's OK, Wendy.' Tim had a dampened dressing on her face and another on her head, trying to control the bleeding. 'I'm Tim and I've got my partner Kat here, plus lots of other people. We're going to look after you and get you out just as soon as we can. Are you having any trouble breathing?'

'No… Where's John? I can't *see* anything. Oh…*God*! I'm *blind*!'

'You've got blood on your face,' Tim told her calmly. 'It's OK, Wendy. We'll get it cleaned up just as soon as we've made sure you're not hurt anywhere else.' His head turned to one side. 'Can we get a C-collar and some oxygen on, please, Kat?'

Kathryn was thankful she was petite. She squeezed past Tim's arms. 'I'm going to put a mask on your face,' she told the terrified woman, after Tim had slipped the cervical collar into place. 'It's just so that we can give you some oxygen.'

A bloodied hand came up and grabbed hers. 'Help me… *please*… Get me *out* of here.'

'Jase, can you put some pressure on this head wound?'

'Sure.' Jason stripped off a heavy glove. 'Don't lean on that door, Goldilocks. Wait until they've got some chocks in to stabilise things.'

'OK.' Kathryn reached into her pocket. 'Put these gloves on before you touch that dressing.'

'Your gloves won't fit me.'

'I keep large ones in this pocket for Tim.'

Tim flashed a quick grin at Jason. 'Kat's the perfect partner, isn't she?'

It seemed an oddly intimate exchange given what was happening around them. Fire officers from two appliances were busy, stabilising the wreck and spreading foam to prevent the danger of fire. A second ambulance crew arrived as back-up.

'Get a blanket down on the ground as close as you can to us,' Tim directed them. 'Set up some gear. We're going to need IVs, another neck collar and more oxygen. Possibly an intubation kit. We can't get to the driver just yet.'

'John!' Wendy's cries and Tim's constant reassurance were almost becoming part of the background now. 'Is he all right? *John!* Can you hear me, darling?' She coughed and then moaned and tried to spit out blood.

'Keep her head as still as you can, Jase,' Tim said. 'It's OK, Wendy. I've got you, love. Kat, can you see if you can suction a bit of this blood away?'

Kathryn lifted the oxygen mask and used the nozzle of the suction gear to clear some of the blood still in Wendy's mouth. At least any internal bleeding from her facial injuries wasn't affecting her breathing, judging by the stream of pleas for help, alternating with the concern for the driver, John.

Tim was still trying to assess the driver of the car. Chocks were in place now and he could lean further into the vehicle. Jason held the high-powered torch higher to try and provide light into the heavily shadowed area of the wreck.

'John? Can you hear me, mate?'

A muffled groan of assent made Wendy sob louder and

try to twist her head. Jason looked alarmed as the dressing he was holding slipped, and Kathryn reached under Tim's chest to put her hands on Wendy's shoulders.

'It's OK, Wendy. Don't try and move. We're getting to John now. We'll take care of him.'

'Pass me another large dressing, Kat. And a bandage. We've got a bit of bleeding happening down here.'

Kathryn could see the deep cut on the man's right arm as she leaned in with the requested supplies. She could hear him groan as Tim packed the dressing into place and wound a tight pressure bandage over it. There was no space or time to apply manual pressure right now but the driver could easily bleed to death if the flow wasn't controlled swiftly.

'Move over a bit, Goldilocks.' Jason's voice was just beside Kathryn's ear. 'We're just going to see if we can pop this back door.'

Seconds later, access to the interior of the vehicle was achieved when the back door responded to the wielding of a crowbar. The gap was still small, however.

'I'll get in,' Kathryn offered. 'I can hold John's head until we get a collar on.'

Tim hesitated. He looked at the local back-up crew.

'They're not qualified to do IVs,' Kathryn pointed out quietly. 'John's already lost enough blood to make fluid replacement a priority, hasn't he?'

'OK.' Kathryn could feel Tim watching her as she climbed into the back seat of the tilted car. Crouching on the door panel that now served as flooring, she was able to reach the driver.

'Hi, John. Can you hear me?'

It was difficult to hear his response over the sound of his wife's sobbing. Kathryn could also hear the 'jaws of life' cutting gear starting up. Hopefully, they could cut away the upper part of the car and extricate Wendy swiftly. Her distress was not helping anyone.

She could hear rapid breathing from her new patient but Kathryn couldn't see well enough to check whether the chest wall movement was equal and her hands were occupied, keeping his head still.

'Have you got any pain in your neck, John?'

'Yeah…and my hip.' The words trailed off into another agonised groan.

'Here's a collar, Kat. I've set it on medium.'

'Thanks.' Kathryn carefully felt the top of John's spine before threading the back of the collar behind his neck. 'I can't feel any deformity,' she informed Tim. 'And the trachea's midline. He's got pain at about C6 to 7.'

'OK.' Tim was clearly busy. 'Wendy, you'll feel a sharp scratch on your hand now, love. Then we'll be able to give you something for that pain.'

'B-pillar getting cut now, Tim.' It sounded like Bruce shouting. 'Jase—keep a hand on that door and make sure it doesn't swing backwards.'

Powerful lights were being set up outside and Kathryn reached for gear that was being passed by the second ambulance crew on Tim's instructions.

'I'm putting a mask on your face now, John. For some oxygen, OK?'

A groan came back as a response. Kathryn tried to lean further over the seat as she saw, to her horror, that the pressure dressing Tim had put on John's arm was already soaked and dripping blood again. She couldn't locate a radial pulse on his other arm, and as she tried to assess how possible IV access was going to be, the car rocked and she fell backwards against the door.

'You all right, Kat?' Tim's query was instantaneous.

'I'm fine.'

'We're clear to get Wendy out now. Be with you in a sec.' Tim's voice got quieter as he turned to people behind him. 'Let's get the backboard in. Cliff and Stick, can you help with a lift, please?'

The car rocked again as Wendy was lifted clear and then Tim was beside Kathryn.

'That arm's bleeding again.'

'So I see.' Amazingly, Tim still sounded calm. 'You put direct pressure on it. I'll get an IV into the other arm. John?' His head was very close to that of their patient. 'You still with us, mate?'

The groan sounded louder now and Kathryn realised why as she heard John asking where Wendy was. The woman's cries had been obscuring a lot of other sounds.

'She's going to be fine,' Tim told him. 'She's on her way to the hospital. We're going to concentrate on getting you out now, John. What's hurting the most?'

'My hip...and my knee.'

Kathryn pressed harder on the bleeding arm. She hoped the hip pain wasn't indicative of a fractured pelvis, in which case John could be losing a lot more blood internally than they could hope to replace. She watched Tim slip a wide-bore cannula into a vein on John's left arm. He handed the bag of IV fluid to Jason, who was still standing close, holding a torch for them.

'Squeeze this, mate,' he instructed Jason. 'We want to get this fluid in as fast as possible.'

'How do you want to extricate him?'

'Flat,' Tim responded. 'Probable neck trauma. We'll put a KED body splint on and then slide him up a backboard.'

'Want the roof off?'

Tim shook his head. 'That'd take too long. Do you know if there's another ambulance on its way?'

'Do you need one?'

Tim nodded. 'Unless one of you guys wants to drive us back to town. It's going to take two of us to look after John.'

'I'll drive,' Jason offered. He grinned. 'I've always wanted a chance to drive an ambulance.'

They had their patient loaded only minutes later.

'How long did that take us?'

Jason dropped his helmet onto the front passenger seat of the ambulance and checked his watch. 'It's been fifteen minutes since we located.'

'Cool.' Tim glanced towards Kathryn, who was sorting out the leads to the life pack. 'What's the blood pressure now, Kat?'

'Eighty-five over forty,' she reported.

'Let's get another line in.' The pressure was still too low. They needed to get the top figure up to ninety at least.

'Are we ready to rock and roll? Do I get to push some buttons?'

Kathryn grinned at Jason's enthusiasm as she leaned into the front compartment. 'I'll push the "transporting" signal.'

'Just go road speed,' Tim called. 'We're going to be busy back here. If you get any red lights, put the beacons on and keep going carefully. Use the siren if you really need to.'

'That's the switch for the beacons,' Kathryn pointed out. 'And this is the siren. Switch onto the top position for wail and bottom for yelp.'

Jason winked. 'I'll only use it if I *really* need to.'

It would be a twenty-five-minute drive to the hospital at road speed. Getting John into the emergency department within the golden hour was still manageable, but his injuries were critical.

'Better get that dressing off his arm and see what's going on, Kat. If we can't control the bleeding, we'll have to use a BP cuff as a tourniquet.'

The laceration in their patient's right arm was deep enough to have flaps of muscle hanging loose.

'The blood loss is fast but steady,' Kathryn told Tim. 'It doesn't look arterial.' She pressed another dressing to the wound, glancing up to locate the spare blood pressure cuff. 'Saline's almost run through,' she warned.

'Get another bag up. We can't cannulate that arm so I'm going to put one in his foot.' Tim was moving to the other end of the stretcher with his hands full of IV gear. 'What's the LOC like now?'

'John? Can you open your eyes for me?' Kathryn held the pressure on his arm with one hand and rubbed her knuckles on his sternum with the other. 'John?'

The groan was faint. Eyelids flickered open briefly and the arm Kathryn was holding moved irritably.

'Responsive to pain,' Kathryn reported. 'I'd put his GCS at nine or ten.'

She wrapped the cuff over the dressing on the lacerated upper arm, fastened the Velcro and then pumped up the pressure. A tourniquet was a last resort to control haemorrhaging but they might not make it to Emergency with this patient alive if the bleeding continued much longer.

New IV fluid supplies had to come from the overhead locker. Kathryn pulled out two bags of saline, another giving set and a pressure cuff designed to fit the bag of fluid and increase the delivery rate. By the time she had hooked up a replacement bag for the first IV, Tim was ready to attach a second bag to the cannula now in place in a vein on the top of John's foot.

Kathryn was reaching over to hook up the second bag when Jason braked unexpectedly. Tim straightened, bracing his feet and catching hold of an overhead handle, but Kathryn lost her balance and would have fallen if Tim hadn't caught her upper arm.

'Ah-h-h!' Her cry was pained.

'Sorry. Did I hurt you?'

'No. I'm fine.' Kathryn regained her balance. 'Thanks.'

She snapped the dog-clip catch through the hole at the top of the bag of saline, then uncurled the giving set and removed the safety cover from the end. 'Shall I hook this up?'

'Yeah. I'll get another blood pressure.' Tim eased past Kat but she could feel him watching her. 'You sure you're OK?'

'I'm fine.'

It wasn't until they were in the emergency department that Tim saw the bruises on Kathryn's arm.

'On the count of three, then.' The doctor holding John's head nodded. 'One...two...three!'

And Kathryn stretched to help lift the backboard from the stretcher to the bed in the trauma room. She was standing directly opposite Tim so he couldn't fail to notice the deep purple bruising on her pale skin as the shirtsleeve was pulled back by the movement of her arm.

Good grief! Had *he* done that when he'd caught her to save her falling?

Surely a bruise couldn't appear that quickly even on such delicate skin? He hadn't gripped her arm that tightly, had he? But the bruises were there, just at the place he'd grabbed her. And she *had* cried out in pain.

'What's the story?' A doctor was staring at Tim.

'High-speed MVA. This is John, who was the driver. He was wearing a seat belt but there were no airbags and there was significant frontal damage to the vehicle.' The report came out rapidly. 'Apparently unconscious when police arrived but he had a GCS of 13 when we got there. It dropped to nine or ten *en route* but has come back up with a rise in blood pressure. Last recording was 95 on 60.'

New leads and monitoring equipment were being attached and staff were cutting John's clothing away. His eyes were open.

'Wendy? Where's my wife? Is she all right?'

'She's right here,' Tim told him. He could see the other bed to one side of the trauma room, a cluster of staff around it.

'She's fine,' the doctor told John. 'She's got a few cuts to her face. There's a plastic surgeon seeing her at the moment.'

'Oh...God,' John groaned. 'This is a mess. I don't even remember how it happened.'

Another doctor had removed the cuff and dressing from John's arm. Blood immediately welled into the gaping wound and trickled down the side of the bed.

'We've had a lot of trouble controlling the haemorrhage,' Tim told them. 'The tourniquet's been on for the last fifteen to twenty minutes.'

'We're going to have to clamp it before we do anything else.' The emergency department consultant tried to swab the wound. 'I can't even see if it's venous or arterial.'

Kathryn had pulled the stretcher clear of the working area and was using a corner of a long bench to make a start on the considerable amount of paperwork needed to document the case. Her shirt was covering her upper arm again but Tim's concern for his partner went up a notch or two.

Her face seemed paler than usual, her mouth was turned very uncharacteristically down at the corners and she stood as though her weariness was more than even the long night's duty so far could have caused.

Tim stayed where he was for the moment. He wanted to watch the emergency surgical procedure thc emergency department staff were about to perform to control the bleeding on John's arm.

'How much morphine has he had?'

'None. Blood pressure was too low until we arrived.'

'OK. Let's give him 5 milligrams now and another 5 if he needs it when we start on this.'

Doctors were gowned and gloved within a minute and a trolley of sterile surgical instruments was unwrapped beside them. John shouted in pain as saline was used to irrigate the wound before being sucked clear. He was given further pain relief immediately but his cry had prompted Tim to look over his shoulder again at Kathryn.

Something wasn't right.

He was sure now he hadn't given Kathryn those bruises. Any marks he might have left would have been red. It would take at least a day or two, possibly longer, for bruising to go those dark shades of purple and blue. But if he had grabbed her really hard, maybe he *could* have caused it. Which begged the question of who *had* grabbed Kathryn's arm. And why?

The answer was as obvious as the bruising, and it was disquieting enough for less than half Tim's attention to be on the interesting procedure in front of him as the severed blood vessels in John's arm were clamped and then sutured.

Could Kat really be in some kind of abusive relationship? Snatches of past impressions flicked through Tim's head at lightning speed.

Like that night in the restaurant with the triple-A patient. Sean had twice interrupted the small team working to stabilise the seriously ill woman at the back of the dining room. On the first occasion he had said something to the effect that it was time they left and there was no need for Kathryn to be involved any longer. Kathryn had ignored him because she'd been busy answering Tim's query about how long the woman had had such a low level of consciousness.

The second time, Sean had been much more assertive. He had, in fact, been an absolute jerk. Even now, Tim could almost hear the irritated snap of someone who had barely been in control of his temper.

He'd had enough, he'd said. Their dinner had been ruined and Kathryn was making a spectacle of herself, crawling around on the floor in public. He was leaving. And then he'd said, 'If you want to stay and play doctors and nurses, that's fine, but you'll have to find your own way home.'

Kathryn had hesitated but then she'd scrambled to comply and Tim had been struck by the expression in her eyes. Maybe the reason he'd never noticed she'd been wearing a wedding ring had been because her eyes had been so captivating in the first place, but it had been at that precise moment that Tim had fallen for this woman. Not that he'd realised it at the time. The reason the memory was still so clear was due to the number of times it had surfaced since.

The expression had made him want to protect her. To hold her close and promise that everything would be OK. That it would always be OK if he had anything to do with it. He'd assumed that her anxiety had been for their patient, and he'd been warmed by the thought that she cared that much.

But what if the anxiety had been for herself?

To outward appearances, Tim was totally absorbed in watching the impressive suturing job in progress in the trauma room. The bleeding had been controlled now and the muscles were being drawn together.

'We've started so we may as well finish the job,' the doctor said.

John's blood pressure was on the rise, his breathing was stable and things were looking much better.

But how good were things for Kat when she wasn't at work?

Another snippet concerning Sean swam into focus. On Kathryn's first day at Inglewood, when he'd been unable to prevent himself asking about her husband. Querying whether the incident in the restaurant had ruined their evening. Even at the time he'd thought Kathryn's response had had a kind of forced brightness about it. Now he could imbue the tone with some kind of warning to back off from private territory.

It had been the same kind of brightness when she'd responded to the query about how her husband felt about her new career.

'He'll cope,' Kathryn had said.

That suggested he wasn't exactly happy about it, didn't it? Why not? He'd be as proud as punch if *he* was married to Kat and she was doing as well as she was in a career she was obviously passionate about.

He *had* backed off, though, hadn't he? When Sean had come to collect Kathryn that first day, they'd given the impression of being a happily married couple despite Sean being clearly so much older. He was prepared to drive her to work and collect her again in his fancy car. He carried her bag for her as though it was an automatic gesture and him calling her 'darling' had twisted something painful in Tim's gut.

'I'm all finished.'

Tim started visibly at the sound of Kathryn's voice at his shoulder and she grinned. 'You're half-asleep, aren't you? You've just been pretending to watch.'

'No—it's been fascinating.' They were up to the skin on John's arm now and he would be left with nothing more than a small scar to show for the life-threatening injury.

'They're taking Wendy up to Theatre. The plastic surgeon is going to do her face lacerations under anaesthetic.'

'Let's get moving here.' The emergency department consultant was stripping off his gloves. 'We'll get a C-spine, chest and pelvic X-ray done. What was that blood-gas result?'

'We'd better get moving, too,' Kathryn said. 'We haven't cleaned the truck up yet and it's in a hell of a mess.'

It *was* a mess. Wrappings from IV supplies, bloodstained dressings, ECG leads and electrodes littered the area, and enough blood had been spattered to make it necessary to disinfect every surface.

'You can go and get a coffee and wake yourself up properly, if you like,' Kathryn told Tim. 'Cleaning is something I'm 'specially good at.'

'No way. I'm not having Laura find out I did something as sexist as leaving you alone with a mop in your hands.'

'Sure? Hey, maybe I should put my feet up and have a coffee while *you* clean.' Blue eyes were twinkling at Tim and Kathryn's smile was mischievous.

And suddenly, inexplicably, Tim felt angry with her.

'Yeah. Why don't you do that?' He turned away, pushing his hands into gloves with enough force to rip the latex. He snatched another pair from the dispensing box fitted to the wall. Kathryn was still standing on the loading platform beside the bucket of hot water she had fetched, and Tim could feel her uncertainty. He had snapped at her and he never snapped at anyone.

'Sorry,' she said quietly.

'For God's sake, Kat, don't *apologise*!' Tim opened one of the large plastic bags designed to hold biological hazardous waste and started pushing handfuls of rubbish into it. 'If you want coffee then go for it, otherwise let's get on with this. It's late. We're both tired and who knows when we'll get the next call?'

'Right.' Kathryn tipped a generous amount of disinfectant into the bucket of hot water and reached for a mop. 'Forget the coffee. Bad idea.'

Except it hadn't been a bad idea and Kathryn had not deserved to get snapped at. For heaven's sake, she had offered to give him some time out and do the job by herself. Why did this unreasonable anger make it so impossible for him to put things right by offering his own apology? He didn't have the slightest justification to feel this way.

Or did he?

He watched as Kathryn pushed the mop into the awkward corner behind the Entonox cylinder.

'How did you get that nasty bruise on your arm, Kat?'

'What?' Even in the current dim light Tim could swear she went a shade paler.

'The bruise on your arm. That must have been why I hurt you when I tried to stop you falling over.'

'Oh…that.' Kathryn was dunking the mop into the bucket again with unnecessary enthusiasm. 'It's nothing.' Her tone was pitched noticeably higher than usual and had that ring of brightness that Tim recognised easily now. 'Just me being clumsy. I walked into something the other day. Funny, but I can't even remember what it was I walked into.' She pressed the foot pedal to close the rollers as she dragged the mop from the bucket. 'I bruise easily, that's all.'

And it might have been all except that Kathryn was lying to him. Sure, you could get a bruise by walking into something, but it wouldn't be a series of bruises that encircled her whole upper arm.

Tim gritted his teeth. He picked up a spray bottle of disinfectant and squirted an area of wall before attacking it with the cloth he was holding. Kathryn's evasion had just confirmed his suspicions and right now he was as mad as hell at her for allowing herself to be in such a situation. What could possibly make her want to stay in a marriage like that?

She deserved so much better.

Like what he could offer?

Yes, dammit! Tim's jaw was aching by the time he'd finished wiping down the metalwork of the stretcher. Kat deserved what he could offer because if he had the chance, he would offer her the world.

How could he offer any less, loving her the way he did?

CHAPTER FIVE

THE night was far from over.

A priority-one call for a potential overdose came through on the pagers just as Tim and Kathryn finished cleaning and restocking the ambulance. Facing a potentially mentally disturbed patient at 4 a.m. was not a welcome prospect when they were both already tired, but Kathryn found herself snapping her seat belt on and reaching for the street map with a sigh of relief.

'You don't need to look it up. I know where the street is.'

Tim's tone was clipped and Kathryn's relief faded, replaced by the misery that had grown markedly over the last twenty minutes. Tim was angry with her and Kathryn had no idea why.

Not that this was an unusual situation for Kathryn to find herself in. Far from it. But she would never have expected Tim to treat her like this. It was a different story at home, of course. Anything could set Sean off and Kathryn had long since given up the pointless exercise of defining the flashpoint. Or trying to avoid the next one. No matter how carefully Kathryn trod through life, Sean would find something to get angry about, and it was a toss of a coin whether she would have to endure listening to him ranting at her or if she would get the silent treatment.

Kathryn slotted the map back into its holder in front of the gear lever and stole a very quick glance at Tim. It would take more than a call to a potential overdose to set his face into such uncharacteristically grim lines. He looked as though they were heading to a jumbo jet that had overshot the runway and ploughed into the chilly depths of Wellington's harbour.

Or maybe it was just a continuation of the silent treatment. A message that whatever he was doing was of far more importance than talking to her would have been. He'd been like that the whole time they'd been cleaning the damned truck. He'd attacked it as though every corner and surface harboured life-threatening bacteria about to leap out at him. He hadn't spoken and he hadn't looked at her, and what upset Kathryn the most was that it had hurt so much.

She'd had no idea that she had come to depend so much on Tim's company. His friendship. To have even the tiniest taste of what it would be like to have that removed was devastating.

Frightening.

And the most frightening aspect was that Kathryn had a suspicion that it was the bruising on her arm that was the real cause of this tension. Had he guessed the real cause of the bruise? She tried to think back. Already well rehearsed in hiding her feelings, she had been careful to project an image of always being pleased to see Sean when he arrived to collect her. Not that he'd kept up the taxi service for more than a few weeks, thank goodness.

She'd always tried to be casual when she couldn't avoid references to her home life as well but, working so closely with someone, maybe it was inevitable that something would slip through. Like that obvious blunder in referring to her home as 'Sean's house'. How much else could have been transmitted without her even noticing?

He must have known she was lying about the bruises. She'd known how false it had sounded even as the words had come out of her mouth. It had been too hard to sound casual because she had been fighting the strong flash of desire to tell Tim the truth. And she couldn't, could she? Because if she told him that, he'd want to know *why* things were like that, and if she told him why he would stop looking at her the way he did so often these days. As though she was special. Attractive. *Lovable* even.

A sharp corner tipped the ambulance to one side and Kathryn put her hand on the door to push herself upright again. Maybe it would all blow over. This was their second night shift. After four days off, surely Tim would have forgotten. The bruises would have faded at any rate. Having a priority-one call was certainly helping. The high-speed dash though the narrow streets of the hilly inner-city suburb required the kind of concentration that would push any personal grievance well into the background. Things were starting to feel more normal, especially when Kathryn reached for the microphone to respond to the radio call.

'Inglewood 950. Go ahead.'

'Roger. This call is to a forty-three-year-old male who is well known to the ambulance service. He claims to have taken an overdose of amiltriptyline hydrochloride.'

'Roger.' Kathryn frowned. 'Did he make the call himself?'

'Affirmative.'

So he was conscious, then. Was it a genuine overdose or someone who knew how to push buttons within the emergency services and happened to feel like some attention or wanted a target for abusive behaviour? Kathryn had experienced both kinds of calls by now but they couldn't afford to make any assumptions. If it was genuine, it could well be serious. Kathryn cast yet another quick glance at Tim, having waited until he had negotiated a particularly tight, uphill bend.

'An overdose with a tricyclic antidepressant gives anticholinergic signs, doesn't it? Dry mouth and peripheral vasodilation that can cause marked hypotension?'

'Yep.' Tim's nod was brief. 'The dangerous side effect of an overdose is the cardiac effects, though. You get a prolonged QRS and PR interval and they can go into a VF arrest or asystole—just like that.' He took one hand off the wheel long enough to snap his fingers. 'They're pretty well stuffed if they go into VF,' he added. 'I've never seen one survive.'

'What's the treatment if they haven't arrested?'

'Volume loading, activated charcoal and whole bowel irrigation. Various antiarrhythmic drugs or even a pacemaker. General cardiorespiratory and renal support.' Tim peered at the street signs as they slowed to cross an intersection. 'What was the address again?'

'Fourteen B Browning Street. I think it's the next on the left.'

'Sounds familiar,' Tim said. 'Was there a name on that pager message?'

Kathryn scrolled quickly through the message. 'Peterson?'

Tim snorted. 'Yeah. I thought I'd been here before. He's a real charmer, this one. Stay behind me when we go inside. He's never been violent exactly, but he can be pretty abusive. We might have to back off and get police back-up.'

Kathryn stayed close to Tim and edged sideways to see past his shoulder as they moved through the open front door and into a tiny and very cluttered sitting room, but Blake Peterson did not appear to present any immediate threat to the ambulance officers.

Stacks of newspapers and magazines littered the floor, along with discarded plates and half-empty packets of biscuits, dirty clothing and rubbish. Several cats were in the room and a dirt tray in the corner gave off an appalling smell. The man sitting in the armchair in the centre of the room gave an impression of frailty. Slightly built, he looked younger than forty-three and his long blond hair and light blue eyes matched the paleness of his skin. He was smiling.

Weird, Kathryn thought, and she shifted imperceptibly closer to Tim.

'How nice of you to respond so promptly.'

'G'day, Blake.' Tim sounded as calm as ever. 'What's been happening?'

'I've taken ten 50-milligram tablets of amiltriptyline hydrochloride. Didn't they tell you?'

'Where's the packet?'

'What? Don't you *believe* me?' The smile got switched off. 'It's on the kitchen bench beside the vodka I used to wash them down. Why don't you send girly there to have a look-see?'

The kitchen door was to one side of the sitting room. Tim nodded at Kathryn and then moved so that he was between the patient and the kitchen door. Kathryn put down the resuscitation kit she had been carrying and stepped into a tiny galley kitchen. Foodstuffs in varying stages of decay covered every surface, including some rotting meat on a blood-encrusted wooden board. A cat leapt down as Kathryn approached and she flinched. Her heart was still pounding as she reached for the foil card and the box it had come from, lying beside an empty bottle of spirits.

She didn't like being here. She didn't even like the reminder of home that handling the drug packaging gave her. She had seen precisely this drug in Sean's bathroom cabinet.

'The tablets are all gone,' she informed Tim quietly, having retraced her steps. 'And the prescription date is only two days ago.'

'Speak up, you stupid bitch,' Blake snapped. 'Don't you know it's rude to whisper?'

Kathryn flinched again, both at the tone and the insult. They were as familiar as the drug packaging had been.

'How many tablets did you say you'd taken, Blake?' Tim's tone was bland. Unprovocative.

'Fifteen. I *told* you. Are you an idiot or something?'

'And how long ago did you take them?'

Blake shrugged. 'Half an hour. An hour. I can't remember.' His eyes narrowed. 'What does it matter anyway? I've taken them and that's all *you* need to know. What are you going to do about it?'

'What would you like us to do?'

Blake stared, clearly thrown by the unexpected question. Tim waited for a few seconds before speaking again.

'How are you feeling at the moment, Blake?'

'You tell me. How *should* I be feeling?' The tone was almost coy and Kathryn caught Tim's eye. She was more and more uncomfortable but Tim's glance was reassuring. He was in control here, it told her. Don't worry.

'Don't *do* that!' The sheer venom from the man in the chair made Kathryn's skin crawl.

'Do what, Blake?'

'Look at the bitch like that. You screwing her or something?'

'If you're going to be abusive, we're out of here, Blake.'

'You can't do that. I know my rights.' Blake's lip lifted in a derisive sneer. 'I'll bet you *are* screwing her. She looks like she'd be good for it. How 'bout it, darling?' Blake pushed himself to his feet with astonishing swiftness.

Both Tim and Kathryn saw the knife in Blake's hand instantly but, having leapt to his feet, Blake made no move to get any closer to them. He stood there, laughing, as Tim ushered Kathryn backwards with a firm hand on her waist.

'But…but…' Kathryn tried to turn as she reached the front door. 'We've left the resus kit in there.'

'Doesn't matter.' Tim pulled open the passenger door of the ambulance. 'Get in and lock your door.'

He climbed in through the back, locking those doors before sliding into the driver's seat. Then he reached for the radio.

'Inglewood 950 to Control.'

'Go ahead, 950.'

'We need police back-up to this address. Patient is armed and threatening.'

'Roger. Standby.' The radio crackled again a minute later. 'Sorry, ETA is fifteen to twenty minutes.'

'Copy that,' Tim said. 'We'll wait unless we're needed elsewhere.'

Kathryn blinked. 'We're going to wait for the police just to go back and get the kit?'

'No. We still need to assess the bastard. He looked steady enough on his pins but there's no way of knowing whether he has actually taken the drugs or not. He'll need to go into hospital for observation and a psychiatric evaluation, and I'm not having him in the back with you without a police escort.'

'You think he's really dangerous, don't you?'

'Of course he is. He's a highly disturbed individual and he's armed. And in case you didn't notice, he didn't look at me once even when he was talking to me. He was fixated on you from the moment you walked in.'

Kathryn swallowed, her mouth feeling suddenly dry. She had avoided eye contact as much as possible with Blake Peterson because the intensity in those pale eyes had been so disturbing. As disturbing as everything else about him. She had recognised the kind of mood their patient had been in so well, and that stirred up a fear she had never allowed herself to name.

The fear that she was in danger from the man she called

her husband. Even now, Kathryn brushed the thought aside as nonsense. Yes, Sean had a temper. He could be nasty, but it was only ever verbal. Or it had been, until the other night, when he'd grabbed her arm to push her out of the room. Out of his sight.

And the funny thing was, he'd started the whole episode by making the same accusation Blake Petersen had.

'You're screwing him, aren't you? You won't give it to me but you just can't wait to get back to work and lay it on a plate for your new partner.'

'That's not true, Sean! You know it's not true. How could I?'

'Maybe you're not such a frigid bitch after all. Maybe it's time I tried again.'

'Kat?' Tim's voice broke through the chilling echoes of that confrontation. 'Are you OK?'

'Yeah.' Kathryn bit her lip hard as she tried to control the wobble in her voice. 'I'm fine.'

'No, you're not.' Tim sighed. Then he reached out and took hold of Kathryn's hand.

He shouldn't be touching her like this but the move had been instinctive and, having made it, he was lost. The connection was way too powerful to try and break. He loved the feel of her small hand within his. It made him feel powerful. Able…and more than willing…to protect this woman from whatever she felt threatened by.

Kathryn didn't pull away. She wasn't exactly holding his hand back but if there'd been even a twitch to suggest the touch was unwelcome, Tim would have felt it. He was far too tuned into interpreting her nonverbal communication to have missed anything like that.

'Some people are pretty scary, aren't they?'

Would Kathryn pick up the inference that it wasn't the patient Tim wanted her to talk about? He rubbed his thumb slowly over the back of her hand. 'You're quite safe now,' he said softly. 'We're locked in here and it's just you and me.'

Kathryn nodded. She attempted a smile that almost worked, and Tim could feel the slight pressure of her hand that told him she had no intention of breaking the contact just yet. Something squeezed almost painfully inside him at the same time. She needed him and there wasn't a damned thing he could do about it.

He drew in a slow breath, his thumb still slowly circling the soft warmth of Kathryn's hand. Wait a minute. Of course he could do something. He could try being a *real* friend and breaking down the barrier that was fencing Kathryn Mercer's private life. Getting to know her better didn't have to mean telling her how he felt about her. It certainly didn't mean an affair was inevitable. These things didn't 'just happen'. Somewhere along the line someone had to make a decision to let it happen. And Tim wasn't going to do that.

Why would he? The way he felt about Kathryn would be with him for the rest of his life. It was way too deep to settle for something as shallow as an affair, and Kathryn deserved far more than that. If he couldn't offer it all, he would offer nothing at all. He might feel angry that she was in a possibly abusive relationship, but he had to admire the loyalty she was showing. He would expect nothing less from someone with the kind of integrity Kathryn had. And maybe Sean had his good points. Maybe those good points were enough for Kathryn to find her marriage fulfilling on some level. Maybe even enough to tolerate what Tim could only see as totally unacceptable behaviour.

'Want to talk about it?' The hand he was still holding jerked fractionally, as though he'd given Kathryn a fright.

'About what?' Now he could see the shadow of fear in her eyes, and Tim felt that squeeze in his guts again.

About your husband, he wanted to say. About those damned bruises on your arm. About whether you're actually happy or not. Something must have shown in his eyes because he could see the shutters coming down well before she eased her hand away from his. Lighten up, he told himself. Kathryn was scared. Vulnerable. A threat from him, at any level, would send her running, and God only knew how long it might take to get this close again.

'We've got some time to kill,' he said mildly. 'The boys in blue must be busy, and this isn't going to be seen as a priority call. I could sing if you like, but I wouldn't recommend it as a form of entertainment.'

She smiled but she didn't make eye contact.

'I could tell you all about apples and pruning trees and spraying for black spot and leaf-curling midges. Even about codlin moth traps. But you'd fall asleep through sheer boredom.'

'No, I wouldn't.'

'*I* would,' Tim assured her, encouraged by finally getting a response. 'Besides, we have far more interesting things to talk about.'

'Like what?'

'You.' Tim's smile was reassuring and he didn't allow any time for Kathryn to feel threatened. 'I've been meaning to tell you that I feel pretty damned lucky that Laura got herself pregnant. You're going to be a first-rate paramedic the way you're going, and not only that—you're one of the nicest people I've ever met. Great partners make great friends, you know?'

She was looking at him now. A steady, almost searching gaze. Tim tried to project friendship rather than the much more intense emotions he had available. The smile was tricky. It didn't feel appropriate somehow, but it was the only way he could make any attempt to lighten the atmosphere.

'Hell's bells, Kat.' The smile became easier. 'We've been working together for ages now and I don't even know what your all-time favourite food is. How slack is that?'

'Mexican,' Kathryn told him. She was smiling, too. 'Tacos and enchiladas and refried beans. And lots and lots of chilli sauce.'

'Whoa! That was no Mexican restaurant I met you at.'

'No.' Kathryn's expression gave a welcome hint of the mischief Tim knew she was capable of. 'Sean hates Mexican food.' The sparkle in her eyes dimmed. 'And even if he didn't, he wouldn't be seen dead in an ethnic restaurant.'

'Nothing less than silver service, huh?'

'Something like that.'

So Sean was hung up on status, was he? Was Kathryn a trophy wife? Had her youth and beauty been the only real draw? Did Sean, in fact, have *any* idea of how lucky he'd been?

'How did you meet Sean?' Kathryn blinked cautiously but it was the kind of question any friend could ask, wasn't it? The silence ticked on long enough to let Tim know he was putting a toe into some dangerous waters.

'He's kind of a cousin,' Kathryn said eventually. 'I met him at my dad's funeral.'

'Oh…' A simple enough statement but a piece of the puzzle that was haunting Tim fell resoundingly into place. Kathryn had loved her dad. You didn't lie on a hill counting stars with someone you didn't love. His death must have been premature. Kathryn would have been grief stricken. Vulnerable. And more than open to the attention of someone who could step into the role of a father figure. 'What happened to your dad?'

'He slipped and fell off the roof.' The tone was matter-of-fact. 'He was only fifty-one. The roof had been leaking for ages but he couldn't wait for it to dry out that time. He was really upset because he'd put Mum's wheelchair in that spot while he was cooking dinner, and the drips were landing right on her head. And, of course, she couldn't move away or even call loudly enough to him to hear her over the television.'

Tim swallowed painfully as another piece of a tragic picture revealed itself. 'Why was your mother in a wheelchair?' he asked gently.

'Multiple sclerosis. She'd got it when I was a baby and had lots of remissions and recurrences over the years. It got worse very slowly but she was in a wheelchair by the time I was fifteen. Dad gave up work to look after her.' Kathryn's smile was wistful. 'They absolutely adored each other. I think it was harder watching Dad's heart breaking bit by bit over the years than it was watching Mum deteriorate.'

'Were you an only child?'

'Yeah. I'd finished my training and was working in Emergency by the time Dad died, but I was still living at home. It was too much for Dad to manage looking after Mum on his own and he always refused to have anyone else living in the house.'

How much time had Kathryn had for any kind of social life? Tim wondered. Probably none. 'How old were you?'

'Twenty-two.'

'How on earth did you manage after that?'

Kathryn's sigh was heartfelt. 'I wouldn't have, if it hadn't been for Sean. He took an interest right from the day of the funeral.'

I'll bet he did, Tim thought grimly.

'I gave up nursing for a while and looked after Mum. I managed to remortgage the house, which gave us enough to live on. And Sean kept visiting. Mum thought he was wonderful. She'd always been so totally dependent on Dad, you know? And there Sean was…to fill the gap. And then…' Kathryn was staring out at the darkness around them. 'Then the bank decided to foreclose on the mortgage and we were in real trouble.'

Tim tried to keep any sarcasm out of his tone. 'And Sean took care of that for you?'

'Yeah. He'd had this investment plan for years and was just waiting for an opportunity to get into the nursing-home business. Our old house was sitting on a perfect piece of land. I helped him come up with the concept of the kind of home I'd want for Mum when it came to that and he actually did it. They built Hillsborough where our house used to be. By the time it was finished a year later, Mum needed round-the-clock nursing care and there was even a patch of her old garden she could see from the window of her room. A cherry tree that she'd planted when I was born.'

Tim was silent for a long minute. Who was it who'd said you couldn't buy love?

'How long ago was that?'

'Five years. I married Sean the same day that Mum moved into Hillsborough. Our wedding was the last time she went to any kind of family occasion. She was so happy that day.'

'Were *you* happy, Kat?' The soft question hung in the darkness for a second. Then two…and three.

'I *was*,' Kathryn whispered.

'But you're not now?'

He could see how painful it was for Kathryn to swallow. He wanted so much to take her in his arms but he couldn't do that. He had no right to…even as a friend. He watched as Kathryn blinked hard. He could see no sign of tears but, then, Kat had given up crying years ago, hadn't she? Why? Because there was too much to cry about?

'I'm happy a lot of the time,' Kathryn said finally. She caught Tim's gaze. 'And the time I'm happiest is when I'm at work.'

Tim held her gaze, barely aware of the gentle smile curving his lips. She was happiest when she was at work. When she was with *him*. And she had talked to him tonight more openly than he could have hoped for. She hadn't exactly admitted that she was trapped in an unhappy marriage, but the inference was there, wasn't it?

It was enough to sow the tiniest seed of hope. If she was unhappy then she could do something about it. If…no, *when* she escaped, Tim would be there for her.

He would always be there for her.

It was just as well the bright flashing lights suddenly intruded into the dark compartment that had almost become a confessional because otherwise Tim might have said something he shouldn't. Or worse, done something he shouldn't, like take Kathryn in his arms and kiss her. He could almost imagine that she wanted him to do precisely that because even the unwelcome brightness of the police car's beacons hadn't been enough to make Kathryn look away from him.

'The cavalry's here,' he said with a smile. 'We'd better go and see what Mr Peterson is up to.'

Taking vital sign measurements on a patient who was handcuffed and had a uniformed police officer sitting on either side of him was a new experience for Kathryn.

Blake Peterson had clearly not taken any drugs that were causing any adverse physiological effects.

'BP's 120 over 80,' Kathryn reported. 'He's in sinus rhythm with a heart rate of 84. Respiratory rate is 16 and the oxygen saturation level is 98 per cent.'

'Perfectly normal, then.' Tim was so good at those 'ghost' winks that only she would pick up.

'Normal' was not a description that fitted Blake even loosely. He had expected the attention he was now receiving and he was thoroughly enjoying it, but Kathryn refused to let the disgusting leers she was being subjected to disturb her. She and her partner would transfer this patient for emergency psychiatric assessment and in all probability he would be back in his own home again in a day or two.

'I was only going to cut up the cat's meat,' he'd told the police smugly. 'I didn't think I'd frighten anybody.'

Kathryn wasn't frightened now. In fact, she felt stronger than she could ever remember feeling. She'd practically admitted to Tim that her marriage was desperately unhappy. A door had been opened that could never be completely shut again. And Kathryn didn't want it to shut.

She hadn't intended saying anything, of course, but that hand-holding had been her undoing. She shouldn't have allowed Tim to hold her hand like that, but the feeling of safety it had bestowed had been overwhelmingly attractive. And she'd added to that feeling by allowing that door to open just the tiniest amount. Finally, someone other than herself knew that things might not be all they appeared to be. Someone who gave the impression that her state of happiness mattered to them.

And then he'd stroked her hand with his thumb and the feelings that had stirred had nothing to do with safety. They screamed danger as they raced up and down nerve pathways that seemed connected to every part of her body. It had been astonishing the way the sensation could travel...and pool deep in her belly to create such a wave of sheer longing. Not that it could ever come to anything, but the bitter-sweet sensation was a new experience and Kathryn didn't want it to stop.

Danger. Sean was already jealous of the time she spent with Tim. If she allowed herself even to flirt with the compelling pull Tim exerted on both her body and mind, it would become impossible to convince Sean he had nothing to be jealous about. And then where would she be?

In a hell of a lot of trouble, that was where. And Kathryn wasn't ready for that kind of trouble. Not by a long shot. Not now, at any rate.

Maybe she never would be.

Tim understood. She had seen such a depth of feeling in his eyes in those last seconds alone together. He was there for her. Whenever and wherever and for however long it took. He wasn't going to say anything. Or do anything, because he loved her and Tim had far too much integrity to challenge what she was doing. He probably had no idea what his expression had revealed, but Kathryn knew.

She knew with absolute certainty what had been revealed because she'd felt something melt somewhere in her soul. Something that was now inextricably linked to the emotion Tim was projecting.

Something identical.

He might have kissed her if the police car hadn't arrived at that precise moment. Perhaps it was just as well it had because, God help her, Kathryn had *wanted* him to kiss her. Even in such a short space of time, the remembered touch of his hand hadn't been enough, and Kathryn wanted to feel the touch of his lips on hers. She'd never wanted anything so much in her entire life.

She'd been kidding herself in thinking that she simply liked and admired and, yes, found Tim McGrath attractive.

The truth was far simpler than that.

Kathryn was in love with him.

CHAPTER SIX

'IS SHE well enough to go outside?'

'Oh, I don't know about that!' The doubtful look Kathryn received matched the new nurse's tone perfectly. 'She had a rather restless night, by all accounts.'

'Did she? In what way?' Kathryn eyed the wide corridor on the first floor of Hillsborough's high-dependency wing. The wall-to-wall, forest-green carpet made an appropriate backdrop for the large potted trees that broke the clinically austere lines of the building's interior. Soft classical music came from speakers set discreetly into the walls and the atmosphere was one of peace. It was easy to imagine the inhabitants would have no trouble sleeping at any time of the day or night.

'She kept calling out. Quite loudly, at times.'

'Really? But she hasn't spoken for months. What was she saying?'

'A lot of it wasn't clear. Diane thought she was calling for someone. Mark, maybe?'

'Mike.' Kathryn tried to push away the familiar feeling of guilt. This was the best place for her mother. The *only* place now, however sad it was. 'My dad.'

'Oh.' The nurse looked suitably sympathetic. 'Well, let's go and see how she is now. Seeing you might be just what she needs.'

'She hasn't recognised me since she stopped talking.' Kathryn's gaze veered away from the young woman at the nurses' station. She found herself looking up at the elaborately framed portrait of Sean which presumably hung over every nursing station in the establishment, along with the other members of the board of trustees. She wouldn't be sorry when she didn't have to visit this place any longer.

'It's hard, isn't it? I'm sorry.' The nurse touched her arm with a professional empathy that didn't quite ring true. 'Let's go and see how she is, shall we? Maybe a short walk outside would be a good idea. It is a lovely day after all.'

'The cherry tree has almost finished blooming.' Kathryn followed the nurse along the green carpet. 'It would be a shame if she didn't get to sit under it this year.'

'They're thinking of putting a plaque on the bench beside that tree—did they tell you? It's been known as ''Eleanor's Tree'' ever since Hillsborough opened.'

'She planted it the day I was born. I had a photograph taken underneath it on every birthday.'

'Yes. I'd heard that you used to live here. You're Dr Mercer's wife, aren't you?'

'Yes.' And Dr Mercer was the major shareholder in Hillsborough. It was enough to elicit a warm smile from the new nurse. The Mercers and their close relative were like royalty here. Important enough to have any request granted if at all possible.

'Hello, Eleanor!' The nurse led the way into the private suite at the end of the corridor. 'Look who's here!'

'Hello, Mum.' Kathryn leaned over the side of the crisply made bed. She brushed a few strands of grey hair from her mother's cheek and kissed it gently. Blue eyes that had probably once matched Kathryn's but were now faded and dull stared back at her. There was something a little different about her mother's expression today, but any hope that the lack of the usual blankness would lead to recognition was short-lived. 'It's me—Kat,' she said softly.

The stare moved so that Eleanor Cooper appeared to be looking over Kathryn's shoulder. It had been hard to get used to, the way her mother appeared to be seeing things, and Kathryn still had to assume she was aware even if she could no longer communicate.

'Sorry, Mum. Sean couldn't make it today. He's off to Spain in a couple of weeks and he doesn't want a backlog of patients to come home to so he's really busy. It's just you and me this afternoon. I thought I might take you out to see the cherry tree.'

Just you and me. That's what Tim had said to her that night in the ambulance when they had been waiting outside Blake Peterson's house. The night Kathryn had accepted the fact she was in love with her partner. Just the two of them. If only…

The nurse pulled a wheelchair from the corner of the large room. 'I'll get some help to put Eleanor in the chair.'

'That's not necessary. I can do it.'

The nurse lifted an eyebrow. 'Lifting people isn't that easy, you know. Especially when they've lost any muscle tone.'

'I'm well aware of that. I'm a paramedic. I lift people every day.'

'Oh.'

Kathryn could see the dawning of something like respect in the nurse's gaze. What had she thought she'd do as the wife of Dr Mercer? Play tennis, have her nails done and 'do' lunches? She suppressed a wry smile. It was what Sean had expected her to do so why should the nurse have thought any differently? It had been a major concession to be allowed the diversion of the part-time employment as a GP nurse. She'd really broken the mould now, hadn't she?

'I'll cross her arms and lift from behind. If you take her legs, we should manage just fine.' Her mother weighed only as much as a child. Kathryn could have done the lift by herself. Settled onto the thick sheepskin that cushioned the back and seat of the chair, Eleanor then had to be strapped in for safety.

'I'll give you a bell,' the nurse said. 'It works on a radio frequency so you can call for help from anywhere in the grounds. Sometimes Eleanor has trouble swallowing. If she starts coughing or having trouble breathing, just press the button and we'll get out to you as soon as possible. Are you planning to go anywhere other than the cherry tree?'

'No.' Kathryn accepted the small paging device. 'The cherry tree is all that's left of Mum's original garden.'

Spent blossoms fell like a gentle, slow-motion rain but Kathryn parked the wheelchair under the tree anyway, beside the park bench.

'Can you smell the blossom, Mum?' Kathryn inhaled the subtle scent and then sighed. 'I love the smell of blossom. Do you remember how I used to make mud pies and decorate them with cherry flowers? And the swing that Dad made for me? It hung from that branch there, just over your head.' Kathryn gazed up at the strong branches of the thirty-year-old tree showing just a hint of green among the palest pink blossom. 'And do you remember the day I picked a whole bunch of blossom and made it into that crown? Dad called me his princess. And then he made you a blossom crown and said you were his queen.'

So many memories. Such happy memories. Kathryn took her mother's frail hand in her own and held it. 'Dad loved us so much, didn't he, Mum? How did you manage to find someone who loved you that much?'

Maybe because she hadn't been married to someone else when she'd met him. Kathryn could imagine that being with Tim would be like the kind of relationship her parents had been lucky enough to find. And nothing at all like her relationship with Sean.

'It was all I ever wanted,' she said softly. 'To find someone who loved me that much.'

Kathryn glanced up, almost guilty at where the one-sided conversation was going. She had never spoken to her mother about her marriage. How could she, when Sean usually accompanied her? When he wasn't there, Kathryn was far too conscious of nearby staff or the possibility of the closed-circuit cameras having audio capacity. Cherry blossom happened only once a year and Kathryn realised, with something like dismay, that this was the first time she had been alone in a garden with her mother for many years. It was also very likely to be the last time.

'You loved this garden, didn't you, Mum? Do you know, I've still got the lily of the valley and some of the other plants I rescued when it got dug up. I keep them in pots in our back garden and I think of you whenever I go out to water them.' They had to be at the back because none of Eleanor's treasured plants would have been at all appropriate planted amongst the succulents and flax collection that Sean's landscapers had favoured. 'One day I'm going to get a lilac tree and plant the lily of the valley underneath it, the way you did.'

One day. When she was free to do what she wanted most. When she didn't have to worry about whether her mother understood what was happening around her and would be made unhappy by her daughter's failure. Would Tim still be there for her? How long would it be? The realisation that she could look forward to her mother's death was shocking. Kathryn's smile was unconsciously reassuring as she reached out to pluck a blossom or two from where they were catching in Eleanor's hair.

'I've got the whole day off today, Mum, so I don't have to rush home. I'm back on a day shift tomorrow. I love my new job. It's real, you know? I hated working with Dr

Braithwaite. I used to listen to his old patients complaining all the time. They only needed to catch a cold and they'd be in there moaning about how dreadfully ill they were. I used to think about you and how you never complained, no matter how bad things got. You made the most out of every good day you had and you just put up with the bad ones.'

Had Kathryn learned that kind of fortitude by example? To simply put up with something she couldn't do anything about? To look forward to and make the most out of any good times? And now her mother only ever had bad days. What kind of hell would it be if her brain still functioned enough to understand without being able to communicate? Kathryn squeezed her mother's hand gently.

'I miss you so much, Mum. I wish I'd told you how much I love you more often. And…and I wish I still had you to talk to because right now I really need someone to talk to.'

Did she imagine it, or was there an answering pressure on her hand? Kathryn closed her eyes. If she could still cry, then this would be the moment it happened. But no tears came. Just a feeling of despair. And then Kathryn felt that tiny pressure again and she looked up to find her mother's eyes on her own, and it really looked as though she was listening. As though she wanted to hear what Kathryn needed to talk about. And why not? She had no one else and Eleanor wasn't about to tell her secrets to anyone, was she?

'I've got a problem, Mum.' Kathryn took a deep breath. 'It's about me and Sean.' She swallowed hard. 'I know you think he's wonderful and I did at first, too. I thought I loved him and that we would have a happy marriage, but it's not like that. It's not even a little bit like that.'

So much had been locked away for so long. Now that the first words had been spoken it was as though a dam had been breached and the outpouring could only gather momentum.

'Even on our honeymoon, I still thought things would be OK. Sean was sorry that he'd hurt me so much. He said it didn't matter. He'd find the right doctor and we'd sort it all out.'

Kathryn hadn't had to think about those shameful months for years now. Ironically, the secret had been hidden by the fact that, to outward appearances, she and Sean were happily married. Why was it in her mind so much more just lately? Kathryn knew why, of course. It was because Tim had held her hand. Because she had wanted him to kiss her. To touch her. But if he did, he'd want more and maybe she would as well and then she'd have to tell him. Far better to practise saying the words on her mother. That way, she might find out whether it would ever be possible to make such a confession to Tim.

'There's something wrong with me, Mum,' she confessed in a whisper. 'They call it vaginismus. It means the muscles go into these horrible spasms and you can't…' An image of Sean came to mind. 'Can't have sex.'

An image of Tim was in much sharper focus. 'You can't…make love.'

Silence fell as Kathryn heard the echoes of her own words. Would it be so terrible to have to confess? Would Tim turn away in disgust? Could anyone love someone enough to get past something like that?

'It can have a physical cause or it can be psychogenic. The doctor I went to said I should see a psychiatrist but Sean hit the roof and said there was nothing wrong with his wife's mental state.' Kathryn snorted softly without amusement. 'I actually thanked him for defending me when we got home but he just laughed. He said he wasn't having some quack feeling sorry for him because he'd made the mistake of marrying a head case. He said I was frigid and then he said, so what? He could get sex anywhere he wanted.'

Kathryn fiddled with the blossoms accumulating on her lap with the hand that wasn't holding her mother's. She made a little pile on one knee and then transferred them, one by one, to her other knee. Very gently, so that the petals didn't fall off the flowers.

'I offered him a separation then. That was about six months after we'd married. Did you know he'd been married before?' Kathryn didn't bother even looking up for any response. 'He said people were already watching us because of the difference in our ages and he wasn't going to be seen as having had two marriages fail.'

Kathryn brushed the pile of blossom from the denim fabric of her jeans. 'We made it work well enough, I guess. I got my part-time job and I enjoyed all the travelling to Sean's conferences and things. I pretended I didn't know about Sean's affairs and I went to all the social occasions he needed a wife for. And I never said anything because I didn't want people to know it was my fault. I felt ashamed of myself and I thought if I'd really loved Sean it wouldn't have been a problem, would it?'

The silence fell again as Kathryn's quiet flow of words ceased. She'd need to take her mother inside again soon. But not just yet. She'd never voiced her misery to anyone and she hadn't come to the most important part yet.

'We could have just kept going for years and years like that, I suppose,' she said calmly. 'But I don't think I can do that any more, Mum.' She bit her lip. 'I think I might have fallen in love with someone else.'

Speaking the words aloud made it seem real. Almost possible. 'His name's Tim. He's my partner at work and he's...he's just the nicest person I've ever met. He's big and solid and he's so, *so* kind. He makes me laugh, Mum. The way Dad used to make you laugh. And I love being with him. I can imagine always feeling like that. Just wanting to be with him. The way you and Dad used to be. I often used to see you just sitting together and holding hands and I never understood what made it seem so special but I do now.'

A gentle smile curved Kathryn's mouth. 'I think he feels the same way about me. He hasn't said anything but I just know somehow. And…I've been having these dreams about what it could be like, you know? Loving someone like that.'

The dreams had started after that night that Tim had held her hand. Dreams of intense longing such as she'd never felt in her life. The thrill of his imagined touch. Love-making that could only ever succeed in a dream for Kathryn and it only succeeded to a certain point when the world would be poised on the brink of explosion and then she'd wake, aching with frustration and sheer loneliness.

'Anyway.' Kathryn gave her mother's hand another quick squeeze. 'I'm not going to do anything about it. I'm certainly not going to let Sean make life any more unpleasant for you.' She unlocked the brakes on the wheelchair and stood up. 'I'd better get you back inside before they come looking for us. They must be serving afternoon tea by now.'

Kathryn paused again halfway across the manicured lawn that led to the front reception area of Hillsborough and the lifts to the first floor. Her mother was peppered with cherry blossom and she'd better remove enough so that they didn't leave a trail on the green carpet. She plucked a few final petals from Eleanor's hair and gave in to the impulse to kiss her mother's forehead.

'Thanks for listening, Mum. I feel so much better now.' She smiled into her mother's eyes and was rewarded by seeing a glimpse of the real woman in the blue depths. Then her smile faded as she saw her mother's lips moving with painful effort.

'What is it, Mum? Are you all right?'

'L-love you.'

'I love you, too.' Kathryn stroked the thin face, her heart breaking. 'I always will.'

'H-he…loves you.'

Kathryn's jaw dropped. Her mother had understood. Was she so upset that she was making the mammoth effort to try and tell her that Sean loved her? That she needed to make her marriage work? She stared at her mother in horror. Would she *tell* Sean about any of this?

But the link of recognition was still there. Kathryn could see the love in her mother's eyes and knew it was simply for her. Genuine love. The kind of love that would never hurt. The kind of love she felt for her mother. And for Tim. The understanding went beyond the need for explanation. Eleanor wasn't talking about Sean. She was talking about Tim. And Kathryn smiled.

'I know,' she whispered.

'Be…happy.'

'I will, Mum. One day.' Kathryn could actually watch as the link was gradually broken. Could see her mother retreating—or being pulled back—into the vegetative state that had become the norm.

'Did she enjoy her little walk?' The nurse was waiting to help Eleanor back into her bed.

'Yes.' Kathryn's smile was merely polite. 'We both did, thank you.'

As though her mother's desire to see her happy had given Kathryn permission to seek happiness, things began to change. Maybe she just opened her eyes to what had been happening around her for so long. Or maybe it was the comparisons that had come into her life so recently. The comparisons were there every day but it was only very recently that they had begun to flash like neon signs.

Like yesterday. They had been called to someone with breathing problems. A priority-one response to a school where they found a fifteen-year-old girl with a life-threatening asthma attack.

'Have you used your own inhaler?'

The girl had nodded, her eyes terrified, her chest heaving with the effort to breathe. She was unable to speak and one of her friends answered for her.

'She used it heaps but it didn't do any good. She's just got worse and worse.'

'Has she been in hospital recently for her asthma?' Tim was wrapping a tourniquet around the girl's arm.

'Yeah. She was in ICU a couple of weeks ago. And she's on pills for her asthma now, too, but they don't seem to be doing any good either.'

Kathryn had emptied the dose of salbutamol into the chamber of the nebuliser mask. She turned up the oxygen flow until she could see vapour begin to billow into the mask.

'I'm going to put this on your face, sweetie. Let's get you sitting up a bit more, too.'

She took vital sign measurements as Tim gained IV access and drew up the first dose of adrenalin.

'Tachy at 130,' she informed Tim. 'Respiratory rate of 46. Oxygen saturation is 86 per cent. Silent chest.'

'Grab a stretcher, Kat. Let's get moving.'

They made it a priority-one trip to the hospital, but by the time they got there the threat of a respiratory arrest had lessened. Repeated doses of both the salbutamol and adrenalin, along with constant reassurance, had been effective but the young girl still needed admission and close monitoring.

Kathryn had completed the paperwork in record time and Tim found nothing to add or correct.

'Fantastic,' he told her. 'Couldn't have done it better myself.'

'Thanks.' Kathryn had beamed with pleasure.

'You're turning into an ace paramedic, Kat, you know that?' Tim looked as pleased as Kathryn felt. 'You handled that case brilliantly. I didn't need to tell you to do anything because you were already doing it. Just as well, too. That was a critical case and it could have turned to custard very easily. I've seen asthmatics like that who are under CPR by the time we get to Emergency.'

Kathryn was still glowing from the praise. 'It was full on, wasn't it? I can't believe that putting dry ice on verrucas used to be a highlight of my working days.'

'It wasn't that bad, was it?'

'It was deadly. Dr Braithwaite's patient population all deserted *en masse* when the new medical centre opened down the road. Only the faithful few stayed and they were almost all over sixty.' Kathryn fished a fresh nebuliser mask from the locker above the life pack and poked it into the bag that hung from the portable oxygen cylinder. 'I'd have whole days doing nothing but flu shots or taking bloods for digoxin levels or telling grossly obese people how well they were doing with their exercise programmes by managing a walk around the block every second day.'

They both reached for their pagers simultaneously as another priority-one callout sounded.

'It's going to be one of *those* days,' Tim groaned.

'Yeah.' But Kathryn was grinning as she slid into her seat. 'Looks like it.'

'It was *so* good.' Kathryn was trying to explain to Sean why she was enjoying her new career so much over dinner that evening. 'Acute asthma that was on the point of a respiratory arrest. A heart attack, a hypoglycaemic coma and an amputated finger at a fish factory. All in one day!'

'I really don't want to hear about amputated fingers while I'm eating my dinner, darling. If you don't mind.'

'Sorry.'

'If it's just the fast driving and sirens that appeal so much, I'm more than happy to give you a spin on the open road in the Beamer, you know.'

'We get to save lives, Sean. That's what's so exciting.'

'Oh, come on.' Sean's smile was tolerant as he reached for the bottle to refill his wineglass. 'You're drivers. Sure, you need to get people to hospital and that's important but that's where the *real* life-saving happens.'

Kathryn was silent for a moment, picking at a meal she no longer had any appetite for. 'How's your presentation going?' she asked, when the silence had become unbearable. 'You leave for Madrid next Wednesday, don't you?'

'I'm not sure if I'll go any more.'

'But you're a keynote speaker!'

Sean shrugged. His glass was empty again and he frowned when the remains of the wine bottle only filled it to the halfway point. 'I can always plead a family emergency. Your mother wasn't looking too flash yesterday, was she?'

'No.' Since Kathryn's recent solo visit, Eleanor seemed to be slipping away quickly. She was unrousable most days and simply lay in her bed. Feeding was being done via a nasogastric tube.

'They've been alerted in the intensive care ward. If she needs life support it'll be available.'

'She wouldn't want that, Sean. *I* wouldn't that for her.'

'You sound like you *want* your mother to die.'

This was very dangerous territory. Kathryn's mother was

a symbol of everything she owed Sean. The reason their marriage had continued past those first awful months. What would there be to keep her here after Eleanor died? Sean's money? Kathryn would be happy to walk away with nothing if it could buy her freedom. She could only hope that the concept of something being worth more than any amount of money would be so alien to Sean he would have no idea how she felt.

He seemed as keen as she was to back away from the topic. He pushed his chair back with a sharp scraping sound. 'We need another bottle,' he declared. 'What do you fancy?'

'I'm fine, thanks.' The level of Kathryn's first glass of red wine had dipped only slightly. Far less than her mood had. She had been looking forward to Sean's trip to Madrid. A whole week to herself. It would be the first time since her marriage that she and Sean had been separated, and the prospect of even temporary freedom had been exciting. And scary. She could do whatever she wanted, couldn't she? And Sean would never know.

Disappointment was enough to make her risk the rest of her evening. 'Why don't you want to go to Madrid, Sean? I thought you were looking forward to seeing a bullfight.'

'I don't think I want to be separated from you for a week, darling.' The caring tone sent a chill through Kathryn. She could feel the tension accelerate. Something was about to snap.

'I don't think I can trust you.' The cork came out of the bottle with a pop, but the sound couldn't be responsible for Kathryn's flinch.

'What's to stop you leaping into bed with that partner of yours? Tom.'

'His name's Tim.'

The quiet correction was ignored. 'Or one of those firemen that are always sniffing around.'

'You're being ridiculous, Sean.' Was he, though? What *would* she do with a week of freedom and the opportunity to spend more time with Tim?

'*Am* I?'

Kathryn could feel the stare. It made the hairs on the back of her neck prickle. 'Of course you are, Sean. You know that better than anybody. If I can't even sleep with my own husband, how on earth would I be capable of having an affair?'

'That's true.' Sean's glass was full again and the danger of a major blow-up seemed to be receding as suddenly as it had begun. 'And how could any of them fancy you in that disgusting uniform you have to wear? You look like a dog ranger. Or a prison guard.'

Kathryn forced a smile. 'It's certainly not flattering, is it?'

'You won't be wearing it for ever.' Sean was looking pleased with himself now. 'I've made an appointment at the IVF clinic for us. For when I get back from Madrid.'

It was impossible not to look horrified. 'I've only been doing this job for three months, Sean. You said you were happy for me to do it for a year.'

'It's more like four months,' Sean responded. 'And it's only a preliminary visit. It's hardly likely to be successful on the first attempt anyway. We may as well get started as soon as possible.'

Kathryn tried to focus on the only positive note in the new conversational topic. 'So you *are* still going to Madrid, then?'

'Don't see why not.' Sean was smiling. 'As you say, it doesn't really matter whether I trust you or not.' His smile became a wryly amused chuckle. 'You're safe by virtue of your virtue, aren't you?'

* * *

Kathryn hadn't needed Tim's smile of approval that morning to remind her of the score of put-downs Sean had achieved in one sitting. She welcomed it as a balm to her self-esteem, however.

'You're looking fabulous, as usual,' Tim said. 'Have I ever warned you how much I fancy women in uniforms?'

The grins of Green Watch fire crew made the flirtatious comment perfectly innocuous. Just part of the usual kind of light-hearted banter that went on around that dining-room table.

'She's married, Tim. Don't think you could compete with someone who drives a BMW convertible.'

'I have attributes.' Tim tried to sound offended. Then he grinned as well. 'It's just that I haven't found anyone to appreciate them yet.'

Oh, but you have, Kathryn cried silently. Tim caught her gaze for just a fraction of a second and she felt her heart swell. He knew he had. If it wasn't for the thrill that such moments of communication could give her, Kathryn would wonder whether the level of frustration was bearable.

'What does your better half do for a crust, Goldilocks?' Jason looked up from the front page of the newspaper.

'He's a dentist.'

'No kidding? Drives a high-powered drill as well as a car, huh?'

Stick punched Tim's arm lightly. 'That's what the chicks go for, Tim lad. Power.'

Bruce was looking thoughtful. 'Did you know that dentists have the highest rate of suicide of any of the professions?'

'That's because everybody hates them,' Jason said confidently.

'Kat doesn't hate them. Not all of them, anyway.'

Kathryn just smiled. She walked past the empty seat at

the table and entered the kitchen. 'Hi, Mrs Mack. How are you this morning?'

'I'm very well.' Mrs McKendry was cracking eggs into a vast frying-pan. 'Be a love and put some more bread in that toaster, would you?'

A burst of laughter came from the direction of the dining table and Kathryn found herself smiling as she dropped bread into the six slots of the commercial-sized toaster. It didn't matter if the amusement was at the expense of her husband's profession. Kathryn felt far too much at home here to take offence easily. The teasing was never intended as a put-down. These men respected her.

Tim trusted her.

He actually said so, later that day. They were first on the scene at an accident that had involved three vehicles.

'I'll check the blue car,' he told her. 'You do the others.'

Kathryn's eyes widened. Tim was the senior officer. He always did the initial triage.

'But...' Even the 'just do it' look wasn't quite enough to convince her.

'I trust you, Kat,' Tim said softly. 'It's time you started trusting yourself.'

And she did. She went to the first car, where the elderly driver was sitting immobilised with fright.

'Are you having any trouble breathing?'

'No. My chest hurts, though.'

'Any pain in your neck?'

'No. Just my chest.'

'I'll be back very soon. Try and sit as still as you can for the moment.'

The exchange had lasted only seconds. Then Kat was at the second vehicle. The distraught young woman in the driver's seat was clearly having no difficulty breathing.

'My baby. You've got to help my baby.'

The infant had been secured in a car seat, but the safety belt holding it in place must have been loose. The seat had tipped and the baby had an area of obvious trauma on its forehead.

'She's all floppy,' the mother wailed. 'There's something terribly wrong with her, isn't there?'

'Tim?' Kathryn had looked over to where Tim was stepping away from the blue car. She managed to sound as calm as her mentor would have done. 'Over here.'

It was the baby that required their entire focus. They were on their way to the emergency department by the time back-up arrived to care for the less critically injured victims. The baby's level of consciousness improved steadily, however, and it was shrieking with distress by the time they reached the hospital.

'I never thought I'd be so glad to hear her crying.' The baby's mother was crying herself.

'Let's get you inside. They're expecting you.'

Kathryn went to a trauma team staff member when they delivered another patient to the emergency department later that afternoon. 'How did that baby get on?' she queried. 'The one with the head injury from the car accident?'

'She's fine,' the registrar told her. 'CT scan checked out clear. She's been admitted to Paediatrics but it's just a precaution.'

'Did I pick the right patient for attention first?' As had become a habit now, Kathryn used any quiet time at the end of a shift to discuss the day with Tim while they restocked and cleaned the ambulance. 'The woman with the chest pain had angina, didn't she? Maybe she should have been at the top of the list.'

Tim shook his head. 'You were quite right. The baby's injury had far more potential to be life-threatening. Any child with a lowered level of consciousness like that is a priority.'

'Gorgeous baby, wasn't she? I love babies that have lots of hair like that.'

'Planning on any of your own?' Tim reached over Kathryn's head to pull bags of IV fluids from the shelf.

'Eventually.' Kathryn was selecting different gauges of IV cannulae. 'I just don't want Sean to be their father.'

The IV fluids were forgotten. Kathryn looked up and bit her lip as she realised the words she had just spoken aloud. Tim's arm dropped in slow motion but his hand caught on the shelf that was level with her face. He was so close to her she could have just leaned forward and she would be against his chest.

'You're planning to leave Sean?' The words were uttered slowly. Almost casually. The expression on Tim's face was anything but casual.

Kathryn swallowed hard. She opened her mouth but no words came out so she nodded instead. Slowly.

The storeroom around them faded to an insignificant background. Where they were right now and what they were supposed to be doing meant nothing. Kathryn was aware of nothing but the expression in Tim's eyes.

'Do you have any idea how I feel about you, Kat?'

Kathryn tried to nod but couldn't. She could only stare, mesmerised by the look she was receiving.

'I knew you were something special the first time I ever laid eyes on you in that restaurant,' Tim continued softly. 'I couldn't believe my luck when you handed me your phone number and asked me to call and let you know how that triple-A patient got on. I had this moment of absolute panic when I thought I'd lost your number and wouldn't have any way to see you again.' Tim's wry smile was very lopsided. 'And then Laura pointed out that you were married and I was so disappointed, you know what I did?'

'Threw my phone number away?'

Tim's eyebrows shot up. 'Who told you that?'

'Nobody. I guessed.' Kathryn smiled. 'You're not great at telling lies, Tim.'

'Neither are you,' Tim countered. Then he shook his head, clearing the distraction. 'It didn't stop me thinking about you, though. I was obsessed. I'd told Laura you were the woman of my dreams and then…then you walked through the door to start working here and I thought, "Oh, my God! How can I *work* with her?" Either she *is* the woman of my dreams and I can't have her, or I'd built you up into such a fantasy that no reality could compete and even if it did, you wouldn't be interested.'

Kathryn was quite sure this was the longest speech Tim had ever made to any woman. She said nothing, in case he hadn't finished, because she wanted to hear every word he had to say.

'It wasn't just a fantasy, Kat.' Tim caught her hand. 'The more I got to know you, the stronger my feelings became. You blew me away with your courage and intelligence. And your humour and compassion for others.'

He took a deep breath.

'I love you,' he whispered. 'I shouldn't be saying this. I *wouldn't* be saying this if I thought there was no hope for a future. But…but if you meant what you just said…then…' She saw Tim's Adam's apple jerk as he swallowed hard. '*Did* you mean it, Kat?'

She had to say something now but her mouth felt so dry. So did her lips. Kathryn touched them with her tongue, her gaze still locked on Tim's. She saw his eyes move, catch the movement of her tongue and then she saw his pupils dilate and the overwhelming desire was instantly contagious.

She couldn't have said who moved first. There was very little distance to cover anyway. Her lips met those of Tim and whoever had wanted the kiss first mattered as little as their surroundings. It was a gentle kiss. The promise of the desire it could fuel or relieve was only a promise. Tim drew back, his eyes closed as though he was in pain. Then he opened them and Kathryn could see only joy.

'That's all I needed to know,' he said softly. He straightened. 'I'm not going to encourage you to have an affair, Kat. That's not something that would be good enough for me. Or you. But I'm here. I'll always be here. For whenever you feel ready.'

Kathryn was ready now. She wanted him to kiss her again. She needed his touch like rain on a parched garden. But she couldn't have it. Not yet.

Sean would kill her if she did.

CHAPTER SEVEN

LOVE.

How was it that something so intangible could be so solid and real?

Kathryn could feel it wrapping itself around her like the softest imaginable blanket the instant she was in Tim's company. He didn't even have to look at her or touch her for her to feel it, but when he did the sensation intensified to such a degree that Kathryn could easily believe that nothing else could ever feel so good. Or so safe.

Even when she wasn't with Tim, Kathryn could pull that blanket around herself and the layer gave her a protection that meant nothing Sean said or did could really hurt her any longer. It had taken Tim to show Kathryn to what extent her marriage had always been a sham, with her acting the part she needed to play in order to survive emotionally. But thank goodness she'd had so much practice because now she was going to need every ounce of any acting skill she had in order to escape.

Her survival no longer depended on keeping Sean happy. Kathryn would never be really living until she could be with Tim. And she would be. One day. It was only a matter of time and Tim was prepared to wait. The temptation to simply pack a bag and walk out of her marriage was strong, but it could never work. Kathryn wasn't prepared to analyse her fear surrounding the repercussions of such drastic action. She just knew with absolute certainty that Sean would not tolerate such behaviour and if there was another way then she would be well advised to find it.

Instead, she helped Sean pack his bags for his trip to Spain.

'I only need to be there for two days. I've cancelled any satellite groups I was invited to attend.'

Two days to get to the other side of the world. Two days there and another two days to get home again. Almost a whole week.

'Will you miss me?'

'Of course.' Kathryn knew the correct answer. 'I'm sorry I won't be there to hear your presentation.'

'Not half as sorry as I am, Kathryn, but it's your loss. You've always enjoyed our travelling, haven't you?'

'Yes, of course I have.' Easy to sound convincing about that one. Time away had always been something to look forward to. Time exploring new places, often alone while Sean attended conferences. Now, however, Kathryn couldn't have cared less if she never took her feet off New Zealand soil again. She lived in a country many people considered paradise.

If she was with Tim, it would be.

'I'll ring you every night. What are you going to do with yourself while I'm gone?'

'I'll be working, Sean, you know that. And when I'm not working I'll be sleeping.'

'You'll have a day off before I get home.'

'I'll visit Mum, like I usually do. I need to spend some time in the garden. I might even do the rounds of the antique book shops and see if I can find something interesting for your collection.'

Sean's stare was unnerving. Unblinking. Like that of a snake.

'We'd better not forget to pick up my evening suit from the dry cleaner's tomorrow.'

'We won't.' Kathryn laid the ruffled white shirt she had

taken from the wardrobe over the back of a chair with a sigh of relief. He believed her. Or if he didn't, he wasn't inclined to make an issue of it. She had a suitable book tucked away for a Christmas gift. Being able to produce it on Sean's return would buy her another hour or two's freedom during his absence. Kathryn didn't want to have to think about doing anything to please Sean while he was away. She wanted to think about her future.

Sean was probably somewhere in the skies between Singapore and London when Kathryn went to see the lawyer whose name she had picked from the *Yellow Pages*. The sensation of actually taking the first step towards freedom was heady but sadly short-lived.

'We get a court counsellor appointed,' she told Tim the next day. 'They need to be satisfied that the marriage has irretrievably broken down.'

'That shouldn't be difficult.'

'Sean would never agree to go.'

'He doesn't really believe that your marriage is good, does he? Surely he can't be any happier than you are.'

'He says he's perfectly happy. Or he did the last time we discussed it, which was a rather long time ago. I don't think he actually cares what it's like as long as it *looks* all right from the outside.'

'So he doesn't care whether you're happy or not?'

'I've never told him how *unhappy* I am. It's not something he'd want to hear.' The silence was enough to let Tim know that telling Sean something he didn't want to hear was not a good idea. 'And I don't think I really knew myself until I had something to compare it with.' This time the silence acknowledged what she had found with Tim. He smiled but Kathryn sighed softly. 'He'll be absolutely furious if he knows I've been anywhere near a solicitor.'

'You can't tell him, then.' Tim sounded very serious. 'I

won't let you put yourself in any danger, Kat. He's already proved he's capable of hurting you physically.'

'I could just walk out but Sean wouldn't let me get away with that. I'd have to apply to the court for a restraining order and they're not going to issue one unless there's some evidence that it's needed. I doubt that Sean would take any notice anyway. He's not exactly...rational when he's angry.' Kathryn could hear the fear in her voice.

So could Tim. 'You'd be safe with me.'

But would Tim be safe with her?

'We could go away. Somewhere he'd never be able to find us.'

'Change our names? Live in hiding?' Kathryn shook her head. 'There are always ways to find people. I couldn't do that to you, Tim, and it's hardly the best way to start a relationship, is it?'

Tim had taken hold of her hand. In the darkness of the garage at Inglewood station, they were as private as they could hope to be at present. Had anyone even noticed how long it took them to park these days when they were returning to the station after a call? Snatched minutes. Precious minutes.

'I don't care what it takes if it means we can be together. You need to remember that, hon.'

'Hon'. The endearment was starting to sound so familiar after just a few days. It was never used in front of anyone but it was as precious as time together like this was. Kathryn could imagine the letters appearing as tiny patches of embroidery on that blanket, adding just a fraction more weight and security as the patches grew in number.

The way Tim stroked her hand when he held it was also becoming familiar. And the sensations the touch evoked were only growing steadily more intense. Sensations familiar enough to conjure up and revisit in the privacy of her own bed, when she could pull that emotional blanket around her like a cocoon.

Desire could be given free rein at those times as well, and Kathryn was beginning to wonder if her 'disability' might only be associated with her husband. If you wanted something badly enough, surely it was possible. And Kathryn wanted Tim.

Very, very badly.

But what if it wasn't possible? What if the discovery that there was a barrier to a normal relationship was enough to taint the way Tim felt about her? If what she had was as good as it was going to get, perhaps she was right to fight the compulsion to move on.

'I need a little more time, Tim. I'll know the right moment when it comes.'

'Just let me know what you want me to do.'

What Kathryn wanted Tim to do was to kiss her, but sitting in the front seats of an ambulance wasn't the right place and disappearing into a locked storeroom late at night might be noticed if there was a call that brought the firemen from their beds. Judging by the look in Tim's eyes right now and the pressure on her hand, he was prepared to risk discovery, but if they started down that path, where would it stop? Kathryn could imagine the whole situation spinning out of control, only to crash and burn. The risk was too great.

'I want you to make me one of those amazing hot chocolates you do. With the melted marshmallows on the top.'

If he was disappointed, he didn't show it. He moved swiftly enough to open Kathryn's door for her. 'Step this way, madam. Your table awaits.'

The hot chocolate smelt delicious but Kathryn didn't manage to get the mug anywhere near her lips. Tim was the first to reach for his pager and his expression was resigned.

'Oh, no! It's a priority-one, isn't it?'

'Yep. Convulsions. We'd better hit the road, babe.'

Their patient was a nineteen-year-old university student and the party going on around them looked set to continue well into Friday night.

'I'm fine,' the student told the ambulance crew. 'They shouldn't have called you.'

'She had a fit,' a young man told them. 'She was unconscious and jerking her arms and legs around.'

'What's your name?' Kathryn asked her.

'Nadia. What's yours?'

'I'm Kat. This is Tim.'

'Hi, Tim.' Nadia smiled brightly.

'Hiya.' Tim dropped to a crouch and raised his voice so he could be heard over the loud music. 'Have you got a history of epilepsy or anything, Nadia?'

'Nah. I'm perfectly healthy. Sorry we've wasted your time.'

'Have you taken anything tonight we should know about?'

'You mean drugs?' Nadia shook her head. 'No way. I don't even drink alcohol.'

The young man pointed to an empty can nearby. 'She's addicted to that stuff.'

Kathryn picked up the can and looked at the energy drink's ingredients. 'There's ginseng and guarana, whatever that is, in this. Plus a bucket load of caffeine. How many cans have you had tonight, Nadia?'

'Only a couple.'

Tim had his hand on her wrist. 'Heart rate's 88 and regular. How are you feeling at the moment, Nadia?'

'Fine. I told you, there's nothing wrong with me. Jamie was just fussing about nothing.'

'I wasn't.' Kathryn could see that Nadia's boyfriend was genuinely concerned. 'She was out of it for, like, at least a couple of minutes.'

'Any health problems that you get treatment for, Nadia?'

'I get a bit of asthma but nothing much. I haven't used my inhaler for months.'

'Any family history of epilepsy or heart problems?'

'No. Can I get up now?' Nadia was sitting on the grass to one side of the party. The music changed and the singer was now rapping at an even louder volume.

'Let's pop you in the back of the ambulance so we can check you out properly. I'd like to see what your blood pressure's like.'

'Do I have to?' Nadia screwed up her nose.

'Please, Nads. Do it for me,' Jamie said.

The look that passed between the young couple made Kathryn smile. She and Tim shared a brief but similar glance as they walked ahead of Nadia and Jamie to open up the back doors of the ambulance. Tim pulled the set of steps down and Kathryn climbed in to put the side of the stretcher down and lift the back so that Nadia could sit comfortably. She dropped the pillow when she heard the shout.

'Quick. She's doing it again!'

Sure enough, the teenager had collapsed and was lying in a crumpled heap at Jamie's feet. Tim and Kathryn moved swiftly and in the time it took to cover the short distance Nadia's limbs were twitching. Then her arms flexed and her legs stiffened. Her breathing sounded laboured.

'Nadia?' Kathryn rubbed her sternum. 'Can you hear me?'

As suddenly as it had begun, the seizure activity ceased. Nadia opened her eyes.

'Oops. Did I fall over again?'

Kathryn glanced at Tim. This was weird. If it was seizure

activity, she would have expected Nadia to be confused on wakening. Drowsy and unresponsive even.

'Come on.' Tim was frowning as he helped Nadia to her feet. 'Let's have a proper look at you.'

'Blood pressure's 125 on 80,' Kathryn reported a minute later. 'Heart rate 84.'

'Blood glucose level is normal as well.' Tim looked down at their patient. 'You haven't been unwell in the last few days, have you, Nadia? Any viral infections? Headaches?'

Jamie was looking rather pale as he sat on the spare stretcher, holding Nadia's hand and watching the paramedics. 'Oh, God!' he said. 'My cousin started having headaches and then fits out of the blue. She turned out to have a brain tumour.'

'Oh, cheers.' Nadia looked far less happy herself now. 'I don't get headaches,' she told Kathryn. 'And I feel fine. I couldn't have a brain tumour, could I?'

'It's highly unlikely,' Kathryn said as reassuringly as she could. The same thought had occurred to her, however. 'We need to take you into hospital, though, so we can find out what *is* going on.'

'But I don't want to miss the party.'

'There'll be plenty more parties,' Tim told her. 'And they'll be much more fun if you're not falling over. Can you get the leads on Nadia, Kat? We may as well find out what her rhythm's like.'

Tim made it sound a mere formality and when Kathryn had run off a strip of what looked like perfectly normal sinus rhythm she went to remove the electrodes. Tim still sounded casual.

'May as well leave them on for the trip.' He smiled at Nadia. 'If you have to miss a great party, the least we can do is offer you the gold-star treatment.'

'Are you going to come into the hospital with us, Jamie?'

'No, don't do that.' Nadia shook her head firmly. 'No point in both of us missing the party. I'll call when I've had a check-up and you can come and get me.'

'I'd rather come with you, babe.'

Kathryn thought it might be a good idea if Jamie didn't accompany his girlfriend. She didn't need any more potentially fatal diagnoses suggested. 'We'll take good care of her,' she promised.

'OK, then. If you're sure.' Jamie kissed his girlfriend and then climbed down from the back of the ambulance. Tim latched the door.

The ride back to hospital was uneventful until they were about two minutes away from the emergency department.

'Pull over,' Tim shouted.

Kathryn was in the back of the vehicle within seconds.

'Look at that!'

Kathryn wasn't sure what to look at first. Nadia was displaying the same strange seizure activity they had witnessed at the party. Her jaw was clenched as tightly as her other muscles and she appeared to be struggling to breathe. Tim was attaching the tubing from an oxygen mask to the main outlet.

A strip of paper was being emitted from the life pack and Kathryn looked at the screen to see what was being recorded. Her jaw dropped.

'She's in VT,' she exclaimed. 'No…it's VF.'

Tim pulled the handle to flatten the stretcher and took the pillow out from under Nadia's head. Kathryn ripped open the package of defibrillator pads.

'Hang on a sec.' Tim was watching the screen as Kathryn reached for the paddles. 'You won't need those.'

'What?' Kathryn turned swiftly. Sure enough, at the end of the irregular squiggle that represented a lethal arrhythmia, a blip appeared that looked remarkably like a normal QRS spike. And then another one appeared. By the time Kathryn had slotted the paddles back into place on the top of the life pack, Nadia's eyes were open.

'What the heck is going on?'

'You've got an irregular heartbeat that seems to be enough for you to lose consciousness. It's come right by itself.' Tim stopped the strip of paper that was now puddling on the floor. 'And we've managed to record it so the doctors will be able to see exactly what's going on.'

Kathryn was still pulling the copy of the rhythm strip through her fingers an hour later, back on station.

'You knew something was going to happen, didn't you? That was why you kept the monitor on.'

'I was running on instinct. I've seen something a bit like this before, years ago.'

'So tell me again. What did you call this?'

'*Torsade de pointes*. It's a ballet term that means "to twist around a point". It's a very distinctive arrhythmia. Starts with an R on T phenomenon.'

'A what?'

'A ventricular premature beat coincides with the T wave and triggers a polymorphic VT.'

'You've lost me,' Kathryn sighed. 'And there I was thinking this was a perfect case to write up for my cardiology case book.'

'It is. It may be rare but it's well worth knowing about and being able to recognise it. It's often reversible because it's drug-induced, and even when it's related to a congenital long QT interval, like in Nadia's case, it's still treatable.'

'She'll need an implantable defibrillator, won't she?'

'Yes. She's lucky we managed to catch the rhythm during an episode. A lot of cases have been known to be diagnosed as epilepsy. The seizure activity is probably just a reaction to the lack of oxygen the arrhythmia's causing.'

'Have you got some textbooks I could read so that I can sound like I know what I'm talking about when I write it up?'

'I can do better than that. I'll help you write it. That way we can go over anything you don't understand as we go along.'

'That would be great. Can we do it tomorrow, while it's still fresh?'

'You mean today?' Tim smiled as he glanced as his watch. 'It's nearly time we knocked off.'

'Today, then. Later, after you've had a chance to sleep.'

'Sure. Want to meet here? Or would you like to come out to my place?'

The silence was tiny but its significance huge. There was no reason why Kathryn couldn't go to Tim's place. And there were plenty of reasons why she shouldn't.

'It's worth seeing at the moment,' Tim said softly. 'The apple trees are all in blossom.'

Kathryn could feel every rapid heartbeat against her ribs. 'We had a cherry tree in our garden at home and it was my favourite place to be, especially in blossom time. But the cherry trees finished flowering weeks ago.'

'The apple trees are at their best. All pink and white like upside-down ballerinas. They smell nice, too.' Tim seemed to be studying the ECG rhythm strip with close attention. He was allowing Kathryn to make this decision all on her own.

'I'd love to come,' she said finally.

She almost didn't go. It was late afternoon by the time Kathryn conquered the nerves that had prevented any real sleep that day.

She wasn't going to sleep with him, she reminded herself, so she really wasn't having an affair, was she?

Except she was…in her head. And her heart. Deception was never going to be her strong point and Kathryn knew if she stepped any further along this track, she was going to have to be honest enough to face the consequences. She was going to have to stand up to Sean. With the kind of strength Tim's love gave her, how could she fail?

Maybe she just needed to believe in herself, and the more time she spent with Tim, the stronger that belief was becoming.

She needed to do that case study, she told herself when she was picking up her car keys. And she needed Tim's help. He was her mentor after all. What was wrong with spending time with him out of hours for some extra study?

Except she could do that at work, couldn't she? They could sit at the dining table and nobody would raise their eyebrows at them using downtime for such a purpose.

She wanted to see the apple blossom, Kathryn decided as she slipped behind the wheel of her car.

Yeah, right. Just who was she trying to kid? It was the thought of being with Tim that was pulling her like a magnet. It was the freedom that Sean's absence gave her that made it irresistible.

Maybe it was her nervousness that made her miss the gateway into the old property on the outskirts of the Hutt Valley. Kathryn knew she must have gone too far and she slowed the car to call to a man walking his dog along the wide grass verge.

'Can you tell me where the McGrath orchard is, please?'

'You've gone past it,' he confirmed. 'It's about a mile back down the road.'

'Thanks.'

'Look for the old wagon by the gates and some big trees. You can't miss it.'

Kathryn waited for a silver Range Rover to pass and then

did a U-turn. Huge old walnut trees hung over the wagon and the gates and she turned up a long, winding drive, trying to take deep enough breaths to slow her racing pulse.

The house sat in a tumble of overgrown gardens that her mother would have loved. Late-blooming daffodils and other bulbs made bright spots of colour amidst a tangle of daisy and rose bushes. Beyond the edges of the garden, Kathryn could see a sea of apple blossom climbing the surrounding slopes of the hilly countryside.

She couldn't see Tim. Kathryn paused on the crushed shell pathway to gaze at a house that looked like it should be photographed for a book on historic New Zealand dwellings. Two-storeyed, the high dormer windows were edged with a fancy wooden lace that matched the edging of a wide bull-nosed verandah running along the front of the house. Paint was peeling from the corrugated-iron roofing, the weatherboard walls looked equally in need of attention and the verandah was crowded with ancient cane furniture starting to unravel, gardening implements and an impressive collection of gumboots.

Kathryn loved it. It looked like a real home. Comfortable and solid and safe. Rather like Tim himself. When he stepped through the front door, wearing faded denim jeans and a saggy, hand-knitted jumper with a length of wool hanging from the end of a sleeve, he looked so much a part of the overall picture she couldn't help her wide grin.

'Like it?'

'Love it.'

'Come on in. I'll show you the rest. Watch out for that bottom step. It's a bit rotten.'

Tim did all the talking during the tour but it wasn't just shyness that reduced Kathryn to staring and making incoherent, appreciative sounds.

'I kept all the old kitchen joinery once I found it was

kauri under all the paint. And I couldn't bring myself to get rid of the old coal stove. I don't cook on it but it's wonderful for heating the house in the winter.'

Kathryn's gaze was taking in the old hutch dresser laden with a collection of antique blue and white china and the row of copper pots hanging in the alcove above the coal range. The feeling that nothing much had changed for the better part of a century added to the feeling of security about this house. Nothing was *going* to change in a hurry either. And neither should it. It was perfect just the way it was.

'The rooms aren't huge but there's plenty of them. There's a conservatory through here but I haven't done anything to it yet. The grapevine Mum planted is starting to take over.'

The vine only had buds on it at present but Kathryn could see that it would become a solid, indoor ceiling of foliage in summer. She could imagine a candlelit dinner at the tiny wrought-iron table in its centre.

'Feel free to pick up a paint scraper,' Tim said as he led her upstairs. 'I'm only up to tread number six.'

The restoration of this house was an enormous job, but Tim seemed quite happy to have taken it on by himself. Kathryn liked what that told her about his level of commitment to things that he considered important.

From the charming upstairs rooms, with their sloping attic ceilings and a view over the top of the closest apple trees, it was also much easier to see the peeling paint of the roof.

'I'll have to try and do something with the outside this summer.'

'It's a huge job.'

'I've been putting it off because it really needs replacing, not repainting, but I haven't a hope of affording that for a while.'

'It's worth preserving. It's an amazing old house, Tim.'

'It's a mess.' But Tim's grin was cheerful. 'A lot of this stuff has been in the family for generations. All those portraits and ornaments and books everywhere. I should clear it out.'

'No. It's part of your history. It's what makes it feel so…homely. This is a real home, Tim. A place for a family.'

'One person doesn't make a family.' Tim turned from his inspection of the roof from the window and his gaze pinned Kathryn's.

He walked towards her slowly. His arms came around her. Big, solid arms. Strong enough to cradle her from whatever life chose to throw at her. Kathryn's cheek rested on his chest and she could feel the steady thump of his heart. As steady as Tim himself was. She felt the soft kiss on the top of her head and then the vibration of his voice in his chest as she heard his words.

'It's only ever going to feel like a home again if you're here with me, Kat.' His hold tightened a little. 'I love you.'

'I love you, too,' Kathryn whispered. 'And I want to be here with you. So much.'

Raising her head, Kathryn's gaze became glued to his lips, willing Tim to dip his head so they could touch her own. But Tim's arms loosened their hold. He stepped back.

'Come on.' He cleared his throat. 'We'd better make a start on this case study of yours. I'm in danger of being seriously distracted here.'

So was Kathryn. It was a real struggle to try and concentrate on polymorphic ventricular tachycardias in general and *torsade de pointes* in particular. Was Tim intending to wait until she was no longer married before he touched her again? Had she given him the impression that she would think less of him if he encouraged her into adultery?

It might take years before a divorce was finalised. Kathryn couldn't wait that long. Why should they? The marriage was over anyway. It had, in fact, never really begun. If she had never had sex with her husband, would that still make an extra-marital relationship adultery?

The decisive snap with which Tim shut the textbook some time later startled Kathryn into dropping the pen she had been using to record notes on the use of magnesium and potassium to control arrhythmias.

'It's going to get dark soon,' Tim announced. 'And twilight is the best time to see the orchard.' He held out his hand. 'Coming?'

Kathryn needed no further invitation. With her hand enclosed in the warmth of Tim's, they left the house through the back door in the kitchen and walked through a large vegetable garden complete with a few hens hunting for slugs. Tim helped her over a stile next to the henhouse at the end of the garden and they set off up a gentle slope between rows of apple trees.

They didn't stop until they were halfway up the hillside and Kathryn realised that the contour had dipped slightly to give a flatter patch of ground. When they sat down in the long grass, they couldn't see the house or any roads. Just a forest of trunks darkened by the fading light and the glow of pale blossom against the deepening purple of the sky. The smell of blossom and spring grass filled the air and the only sound was their slightly quickened breathing from the uphill walk. And Kathryn's hand was still being held. She squeezed Tim's fingers.

'This is way better than my cherry tree.'

'This is where I used to hide when I was a kid.'

'Did you make mud pies and decorate them with blossom?'

'No. I never thought of doing that. Must be a girl thing. I used to drive my toy truck around, though.'

'I don't suppose you ever made a blossom crown either, and pretended to be a princess.'

'No.' Tim's expression was unreadable in the twilight. He pushed himself to his feet. 'But it's time I did, if you ask me.'

He snapped the soft ends from the branches of the nearest tree. His twisting and joining was inexpert but he managed a rough circle and only half the blooms had fallen off. With a lopsided smile he knelt to place the crown on Kathryn's head.

'Here you go, princess.'

He adjusted the position of the crown and then smiled into her eyes. This time his head *did* dip and Kathryn barely registered the wreath slipping from her head as their lips touched. It was the briefest touch to begin with and then Tim's lips were dancing slowly over her face, dropping soft kisses on her forehead, on her neck below her ears, the tops of her cheeks and the corners of her mouth.

'I love you,' he whispered between kisses. 'I want you.'

In answer, Kathryn reached up, burying her fingers in the soft, dark curls on his head as she steered his lips back to meet hers full on. It was Kathryn who parted her lips first and then sent the tip of her tongue to touch his bottom lip before venturing further. And Tim's response was as passionate as she had known it would be. It fuelled her own desire and made her hands wander to test the shape of his body in the same way Tim's hands were shaping hers.

The touch on her breasts even through her clothing made a soft sound of need escape her lips, and Tim raised his head.

'I can stop,' he said quietly. 'If that's what you want.'

Kathryn swallowed painfully. 'It's not what I want,' she said. 'But…'

Tim sat up. His hands balled into fists and his eyes were closed. 'I know,' he groaned. 'I understand.'

'No, you don't.' Kathryn struggled to a sitting position. 'It's not that I don't want to, Tim.' She reached out and touched his knee. 'It's that I'm not sure that I *can*.'

Tim just nodded. 'We'll have to wait,' he said. 'It won't kill me.' He gave Kathryn a shaky smile. 'It just feels like it will.'

Kathryn felt far more shaky than Tim's smile. She loved this man so much. He deserved honesty if nothing else.

'It's not because I'm still married,' she said very quietly. 'It's because I've never...'

'Had an affair?'

'Made love.' Kathryn's voice was the tiniest whisper. It fell into a silence so complete she could imagine she had only thought the words rather than spoken them aloud.

'You mean it was just sex with Sean?' Tim's hand had found hers again. She could feel the strength flowing into her. Giving her courage.

'I've never had sex with Sean.'

The silence was even more profound. Kathryn could feel the beginnings of a shiver starting deep within her. The chill of potential rejection perhaps?

'I couldn't,' she heard herself continue. 'And after a while we just stopped trying. The doctor told me I had a severe case of vaginismus. Psychogenic. Sean decided it wasn't worth the bother of trying to cure me when there were plenty of willing partners available.'

Tim's voice was tight. Almost strangled. 'Were you a virgin when you got married?'

Kathryn's snort was self-deprecating. 'I still am, I guess.'

'Did he hurt you? The first time?'

Kathryn nodded. 'He didn't set *out* to hurt me, though.'

Tim pulled her into his arms. He rocked her. And when

he spoke he sounded very, very angry. 'I'd like to kill the bastard,' he said softly. 'How could he do that to you?'

'But it was my fault. I'm the one who has something wrong with me.'

'Baby, there's nothing wrong with you.' He was still rocking Kathryn as he kissed her head again. 'Whatever the reason, you weren't ready that first time. Sean must have made it a thousand times worse.'

'I was scared,' Kathryn admitted. 'And I don't think I was ever sexually attracted to him really. Maybe I saw him as some kind of father figure.'

'Are you sexually attracted to me, babe?'

'You know I am, Tim. I'm just scared that I'll disappoint you.'

'You could never do that, Kat.' Tim traced the outline of her face with gentle fingers. 'If you only existed from the waist up, I'd still love you. I'd still want to be with you.' His smile was as gentle as his touch. 'The sex would have to be somewhat creative, though, wouldn't it?'

'I love you, Tim. I want to be with you in every way possible. I'm just not sure that making love *is* possible.'

Tim's eyes were as dark as the surrounding night. 'Do you want to find out?'

Kathryn caught the finger tracing her bottom lip and kissed it. 'Yes,' she whispered. 'I think I do.'

The hand dropped to stroke her breast. It traced a line across her belly and the shiver that Kathryn gave had nothing to do with any chill.

'Are you sure?'

Tim's hand rested on the zip of her jeans for a split second and the heat building inside Kathryn made her wonder if her skin would erupt in tiny flames. Nothing existed in that moment but the love they shared. She reached for Tim, to pull him closer as she lay down in the long grass again.

'I'm sure,' she told him. 'I've never been more sure in my life.'

CHAPTER EIGHT

MIRACLES *could* happen.

Kathryn turned to let the rain of hot water caress her back as she reached for the soap. The touch of her own lathered hands, even the touch of the water was enough to keep her level of awareness at a peak she hadn't known existed.

She had never felt this alive.

Every square centimetre of her skin had been sensitised. Woken from a place that she'd only glimpsed in her dreams. Kathryn could feel something like a blush heat her cheeks as she remembered she probably didn't possess a square centimetre of skin that Tim hadn't touched with his gentle hands, or his lips…or his tongue. It was hardly a surprise to feel her breasts swelling and her nipples hardening as she rotated slowly to rinse the suds from the front of her body.

It was only an hour since she'd left Tim's bed. She should be feeling exhausted because they hadn't slept a wink. Instead, she felt energised. Capable of achieving anything she desired. *Alive.*

And scared.

Kathryn felt so different. Every movement of her body was a reminder of how much had changed. She towelled herself dry a little more carefully than usual. There were tender areas but the discomfort was as welcome as the new feeling of energy. She had expected love-making to be impossible, but Tim had been so gentle and slow that first time in the orchard and she had wanted him so much that in the end it had been Kathryn who had demanded penetration. And fulfilment.

Physical pain had been an expectation but there had been none. The overwhelming emotional pain had been unexpected. A grief, almost, for what she had been denied for so many years. A joy that she had found this and a fear that she couldn't simply embrace it with any confidence that it could happen again. She had a journey to embark on now that was more terrifying than any she had ever faced before.

Kathryn had to escape a loveless union with a man who had no intention of letting her go.

Picking up her discarded clothing from the bathroom floor, Kathryn buried her nose in the armful, knowing that she would catch the scent of Tim and another reminder of the hours they had just spent together. Hoping it would give her the strength to face the day because it was going to be a long, hard one. It was still only 6 a.m. but within an hour she would have to be at the airport waiting to greet Sean on his arrival home.

Would he see what had to be stamped on her face? On her body? Would the inevitable confrontation begin right there at the airport? No. Sean never lost control in public. He would wait until he was in the privacy of his own home. He might be tired after his long, international flight so he could well shower and then sleep for hours. She would have to find a way to fill her day and prepare herself for what had to come.

The beeping of her cellphone interrupted Kathryn's passage through the kitchen on her way to the laundry. Heart thumping, she reached to read the text message. Had Sean's flight landed early?

Luv u. The number was Tim's.

Tears pricked and then swamped her vision as Kathryn tried to push the buttons to send a reply. She sniffed and scrubbed at her face, smiling through her tears. Last night had been the first time in so many years that she'd cried.

Cradled in Tim's arms in that overwhelming flood of emotion after their first coupling, she had thought all the accumulated years of unhappiness had been washed clear. But here she was again, with tears on her cheeks at the joy created by even such a remote connection to the man she loved.

Heavens! If she kept bursting into tears so easily, Sean would have no difficulty gaining control of their situation. Another sniff and the smile won. The keypad became clear.

Luv u 2

Her phone beeped again seconds later. *Gd luk 4 2day*

Thnx, she sent back. *I'll need it*

Call if u need me

OK

When the phone rang as soon as she'd sent the last message, Kathryn answered it without hesitating even long enough to look at the caller display screen. It had to be Tim.

'Hi, babe,' she said softly. Any shyness she was feeling evaporated instantly in the silence she heard and was replaced by a nasty chill spreading from the base of her spine. If it wasn't Tim, then it had to be…

'Mrs Mercer?'

'Speaking.' The voice was that of a woman.

'It's Ellen James here, Mrs Mercer. From Hillsborough Hall?'

'Oh?' Kathryn was taking a deep breath, still shaky from the narrow escape. Thank God it hadn't been Sean on the other end of the line.

'I'm afraid I have some bad news.' The sympathetic voice seemed to fade into patches of static so that many of the words simply vanished. 'Your mother…in the night…very peacefully…sending a car.'

Kathryn was still standing in the same spot, clutching her phone, when the doorbell sounded ten minutes later.

'It's very kind of you,' she told the chauffeur distantly. 'But I'm supposed to be collecting my husband from the airport this morning.'

'We'll take care of that,' the elderly man told her. 'They're expecting you at Hillsborough, Mrs Mercer. Everything's being arranged.'

Kathryn nodded. Anything else that needed coping with right now would just have to wait. She couldn't think due to the curious buzzing in her head.

'Is there anything you want to bring with you?' The chauffeur had a very kind face. 'Is that your handbag?'

Kathryn nodded again. His touch on her arm was welcome. She felt lost and so very alone.

'Come with me, love. We'll take care of you. Anything else you need?'

'My phone.' It was the only potential link to a haven that had taken her on a dreamlike unreality. A person and place that seemed to be getting further from her reach with every passing minute. 'I need my phone.'

The glances being exchanged between the senior members of Hillsborough's staff were wary.

'You're welcome to read the nursing notes, Dr Mercer. I'm sure you'll find that your mother-in-law received the same high standard of care than any of our patients can expect.'

'Eleanor Cooper was not just "any" patient. As you well know. Precisely what time was her death discovered?'

'Six a.m.'

'And how long had it been since she was last checked?'

'She had hourly observations done overnight. As usual. There had been no indication at 5 a.m. of any deterioration in her condition.'

'She should have been on continuous cardiac monitoring.

I find it unacceptable that she died without anyone even *noticing*.'

'Leave it, Sean.' Kathryn's calm tone surprised everyone, including herself. 'There's really no point when Mum was under a "do not resuscitate" order.'

'She wasn't,' Sean snapped. 'I took care of that.'

Kathryn's sigh was almost peaceful. This was a battle she no longer had to fight. 'Life support and intensive care would have been the last thing she would have wanted. Dying peacefully in her sleep was exactly what I would have wished for her.'

'You wished for your mother's death?'

More glances were exchanged and Kathryn could feel the sympathy she had been enveloped in until her husband had arrived at Hillsborough a few minutes ago. It gave her strength. 'Mum was terminally ill with an incurable disease, Sean. She's been in a coma for more than two weeks. She wasn't really alive at all, was she?'

'Her condition could have improved. If she'd been cared for well enough she might have enjoyed another remission and regained some quality of life for years.'

'She's dead, Sean.' The words were harsh. Flat. But Sean wasn't grieving for someone he'd loved, was he? Any anger at the loss he was suffering was because the major component of his hold over Kathryn was gone. He could no longer threaten to let her mother end her days if not on the streets then in an overcrowded and under-resourced state-funded home.

Kathryn pushed back stray locks of her hair which she hadn't bothered restraining in any way that morning. It was hard to believe that only hours ago Tim had been combing his fingers through the soft tresses…using handfuls of her hair to tilt her head to meet his kisses.

Any guilt she had expected to feel in facing her husband

was simply not there. Grief had taken its place. And part of that grief was because she couldn't tell her mother that she had finally found real happiness and that she was ready to fight any battle necessary in order to keep it. A soft smile tugged unexpectedly at her lips. Maybe her mother had sensed her happiness. Maybe that was why she had chosen this particular day to slip away.

Sean was staring at Kathryn with a mixture of disbelief and disgust on his features.

'I'd like to spend some time with my mother.' The formalities of the death had already been attended to, but the brief visit Kathryn had been granted so far was not nearly enough.

'Of course.' The matron had clearly been expecting her request. 'Everything's ready for you. You can stay just as long as you wish.'

Sean was nodding now. 'I'll come with you, darling.' He put his hand on Kathryn's arm.

'No.' Kathryn stepped to one side. Such a touch was only for public display and it made her skin crawl. She knew now what it was like to be touched with genuine love. Sean would never touch her again if she could prevent it. 'I want to be alone with my mother.'

The new silence was charged with tension and Kathryn realised that this was probably the first time she had ever taken a public stand against any preference of Sean's, apart from that night in the restaurant when she had ignored his demand that she leave the care of that patient to the paramedics. Had that been the moment when any power Sean had over her had begun to disintegrate? Had it been the career she had been pulled so strongly towards or had something in her soul recognised Tim's importance long before she had herself?

She would, no doubt, pay for this stand later, but she

couldn't have cared less. The confrontation was going to happen and a fight about her public rejection of his comfort could well be the perfect opportunity to tell him she was leaving. The prospect didn't even excite any fear. Kathryn was quite numb right now. All she wanted was a private time to say goodbye to her mother. Maybe Eleanor couldn't hear her but it was still an opportunity to open her heart to someone who, until very recently, had been the only person she could trust enough to return the love she offered.

'It's the grief.' Sean's overly tolerant tone followed Kathryn down the quiet corridor. 'It does strange things to people. Kathryn's obviously not herself at the moment, which is perfectly understandable.'

Being 'not herself' was a welcome reprieve over the next couple of days. Kathryn's world had shattered in more ways than one, and Sean seemed to be stepping as warily as she was herself. Kathryn found she could demand things with an increasing expectation of achievement. Small things compared to what needed to happen in her life, but her confidence was building.

'No. I don't want a lavish funeral for Mum, Sean. A quiet ceremony in Hillsborough's chapel will be fine.'

'No headstone. I want Mum's ashes scattered under the cherry tree and the plaque they were talking about for that bench seat.' The seat she had been sitting on when she'd told her mother about her love for Tim.

'No. I don't want company. I'm going for a walk.'

The winding tracks of Mount Victoria's bush-covered slopes behind the house led to a memorial that gave a superb view over the city. It also gave excellent cellphone coverage and an opportunity for a private conversation.

'How was the funeral, hon?'

'Strangely enough, it was lovely. We played her favourite

songs and all her friends from years ago were there and had something nice to say about her.'

'I wish I could have been there for you.'

'I wish you could have, too. I wish Mum could have met you. I'm just glad she knew about you…sort of.'

'How's it been…otherwise?'

'Weird.' Kathryn shivered a little in the cold wind and walked away from the group of tourists disembarking from a bus. 'Sean's hardly speaking to me. He didn't come home at all last night and he's drinking a lot more than usual. I suspect he knows as well as I do that things are changing.'

'But he hasn't said anything?'

'No. Neither have I. Everything's been on hold until we got the funeral over with. Maybe tonight.'

'Be careful, hon.'

'I will. I'll be out of the house nice and early tomorrow anyway. I'm coming back to work.'

'Already? Are you sure you want to? They can get someone in to cover for you for a few days, you know.'

'I want to be at work, Tim.' Kathryn smiled and lowered her voice despite there being no one close enough to hear her. 'It's been three days since I've even seen you. Text messages aren't the same.'

'Are you remembering to erase them?'

'Yes. I'm not letting my phone out of my sight, anyway. I don't know how I would have got through the last few days without you.' Kathryn turned away from the memorial as a large silver vehicle pulled into the last available parking space nearby. 'I'd better head home,' she said reluctantly. 'It's freezing up here.' She smiled again. 'Love you.'

'Love you, too, babe. Call me when you can and…and don't say anything tonight if it looks dodgy. We'll talk tomorrow. Make some plans.'

'Sure.' Kathryn knew that Tim had been wise in suggesting that Kathryn leave him well out of any reasons she wanted to leave Sean. She needed to keep things as simple as possible and focus on the first goal of actually leaving her marital home.

'Kat?'

'Mmm?'

'I'm not sure I like you walking on those bush tracks by yourself.'

'I'll be careful.'

There were plenty of people on the tracks at this time of day. A woman walking two Yorkshire terriers said hello as she passed Kathryn on her way uphill and a man jogged past going downhill. He reappeared ten minutes later, retracing his steps with obvious effort, and Kathryn gave him an encouraging smile.

'Looks like hard work,' she called.

The lack of any acknowledgement might have been what prompted her to glance over her shoulder as she reached the end of that straight section of the track. Her surprise at seeing the jogger standing still and staring back at her was enough to make Kathryn quicken her pace. Maybe it wasn't so safe being out here alone, but she wouldn't need the walks for the next few days because she would be able to talk to Tim at work.

By the time her four days at work were over, it was quite possible that her life could have changed even more and she wouldn't be heading back to Sean's house as she was at present, with the feeling of tension increasing steadily with every step.

'You can't go back to work tomorrow.'

'I don't see why not.'

'I've made an appointment for us at the IVF clinic. It wasn't very convenient for them after cancelling yesterday's appointment at such short notice, but they've been very accommodating.'

'You should have discussed it with me first, Sean.'

'I was trying to look after things that weren't associated with your mother's funeral, seeing that you were so determined to shut me out of having anything to do with that.' Sean dropped a handful of ice cubes into his tumbler and then jerked the crystal stopper from the decanter holding his favourite whiskey. 'After all I've done for your mother all these years. I only did my best, you know, Kathryn. For your mother *and* you.'

Sean's tone was genuinely puzzled, his gaze almost appealing. For an instant Kathryn was reminded of why she had married him. He was, or had been, quite capable of being a decent person. The turmoil of the last few days was enough to remind her of what it had been like when her father had died, too. What a relief it had been to have someone who wanted to take control. But Sean's ability to control had never been simply protective or supporting. His motivation had always been selfish.

'She wouldn't have been in a place anything like Hillsborough if it hadn't been for me.'

'No,' Kathryn agreed. The hardening of Sean's tone was enough to chase any poignant memories away. 'I'm very grateful that she had the standard of care she did have.'

'You've got a funny way of showing it.'

'Why? Because I'm going back to work?'

'Precisely. People will think you don't give a damn that your mother has just died.'

'A lot of people use their work as a distraction from grief. It's a form of comfort, sticking to a known routine.' And the source of the real comfort Kathryn had craved for the last few days would be sharing that routine. 'Of course I give a damn,' she continued. 'That's why I *need* to work. I couldn't bear just sitting around thinking about it all the time.'

'A baby would be a much better distraction than your job.' Sean made her career sound like some hobby of questionable value. 'And just remember, you only have your job because I *allow* you to have it.'

She must have been so naïve to have ever thought she loved this man. Did he really think that anyone other than a child would accept such a relationship? Of course he did and she had to take some responsibility for encouraging him to think that way by her lack of rebellion. But she was growing up finally. She had Tim to thank for giving her the self-esteem she had never gathered until now. She *was* worth more than Sean would ever give her credit for. She deserved more than this.

'I don't want to even think about having a baby right now, Sean. It's the worst possible time.'

'It's the best time, if you ask me.' Sean tossed off the last of his drink and moved back towards the drinks cabinet. 'In the midst of death is life. Or is that the other way round?' Sean smiled at the stream of amber liquid covering ice that hadn't had time to melt. 'Whatever. A baby is what we need, Kathryn. It's what we've always needed to make this marriage work.'

'No!' The word came out far more vehemently than Kathryn had intended. Here was the opportunity to tell Sean that she would never have his baby. That the marriage could never 'work' in any sense. The look she was receiving tangled the words in her head so that they had no hope of escaping, however. She knew that look and no matter how much self-esteem she could gather, it would never lose its power to frighten her. She tore her gaze away and stared at her hands. 'I mean...just give me some time, Sean. I've got too much on my mind right now.'

'Such as?' The query was snapped back in a tone that Kathryn knew as well as the look accompanying it. Sean was itching for an outlet. Three days with no display of anger was probably going to be it as far as any personal records went.

Kathryn suddenly felt very, very tired. 'For God's sake, Sean. I buried my *mother* today. Just give me a—'

The strident ringing of the doorbell interrupted Kathryn's sentence. Sean raised an eyebrow.

'Are you expecting visitors, Kathryn? One of your buddies from *work*, maybe?'

'Of course not. It's probably just more flowers being delivered.'

The house was already awash with giant bouquets that disrupted the minimalist lines of the décor and added to Kathryn's feeling of displacement. In fact, things felt so unreal at the moment she was hardly surprised to open the front door and find two uniformed policed officers at the entranceway. They were neatly framed by the topiary buxus plants on either side of the Italian tiles they were standing on, and Kathryn found herself almost smiling at the bizarre symmetry of the picture.

'Is this the home of Dr Sean Mercer?'

'Yes.' Kathryn stared at the ID card as she listened to the detective introduce himself and his partner. It was too late for any bad news concerning her mother, and the only other person that really mattered was Tim. She bit her lip. 'What's happened?'

'Is Dr Mercer at home?'

'Yes, he is.'

'We'd like to speak to him if that's possible.'

'Of course.' Respect for authority was ingrained in Kathryn. Sean, however, looked anything but co-operative at the intrusion.

'This is not a convenient time,' he informed the police officers. 'I've just got home from the funeral of a close family member.'

'I'm sorry to hear that, sir.'

'Maybe you could come back some other time.'

'This won't take long. You're a rather key person we need to speak to regarding a potential homicide case.'

Kathryn sank onto the edge of a cream leather armchair in the corner of the formal lounge. A homicide? *Murder?*

'What?' Sean's look suggested that the detective's IQ was unlikely to climb from single figures.

'A body has been discovered in the last couple of days, Dr Mercer. In an isolated part of the Rimutaka Ranges.'

'What on earth could that possibly have to do with me?'

'The body has been identified as Jillian Mercer. Your...' The detective cast a speculative glance in Kathryn's direction. 'Your wife?'

'Ex-wife.' Sean's tumbler jerked just enough to spill a few drops of amber liquid onto the rich burgundy carpet. 'Good Lord!' Sean was visibly collecting himself as he drained his glass. 'Perhaps you'd better sit down after all.'

He stood up as the visitors accepted the invitation. 'Can I get anyone a drink?'

'No. Thank you.'

Kathryn stared at Sean as he walked to the cabinet anyway. Jillian. She had known Sean had been married before, but hearing her name for the first time created an odd feeling of sympathy for her predecessor that had nothing to do with an untimely demise. Distractedly, Kathryn wondered if the woman had preferred being called Jill and decided that if she had, Sean would probably have always called her Jillian. Sean had once said that the marriage had been a mistake. Why? Because Jillian had managed to escape?

'What makes you think that this could be homicide?'

'The body was partially covered. Whether a slippage buried her or uncovered a shallow grave is uncertain at this point. The clothing she was wearing doesn't suggest she was planning a tramping expedition.'

'So there's no real evidence of foul play, then?'

The detective had opened a notebook. 'When did you last have contact with your ex-wife, Dr Mercer?'

Sean shrugged. 'It's at least seven years since our marriage broke up.'

'And you've remarried?' The detective glanced at Kathryn again.

'Five years ago. *If* that's any of your business.' The decanter was empty by the time Sean put it down and Kathryn frowned. Surely it had been full when they'd arrived home this afternoon? When she had refused a drink and gone out pleading the need for some fresh air instead?

'I'm afraid it is, sir. Jillian's family say they've had no contact with her for over seven years. Since she married you, in fact.'

'That was their choice. They disapproved of the marriage.'

Kathryn tried to release the tight grip she had on the upholstery of her seat. Why had they disapproved? Sean had turned on the charm with both herself and her mother, and Eleanor had thought him wonderful. Had being sick and vulnerable made enough of a difference?

'She was never reported as missing.'

'She wasn't "missing" as far as I'm concerned. She walked out of our marriage and I had no further contact. My solicitor took care of all the paperwork concerning the separation and divorce. I just signed on the dotted lines.'

'We'll need the name of your solicitor.'

'He's dead.' Sean clearly felt in control of this interview

now. Kathryn could see it in his smile. 'A heart attack, I believe. He died four or five years ago.'

'We'll still need his details.'

'No problem. In fact, I can find them for you now.' If Sean's gait was at all unsteady as he walked from the room, he covered it well. He returned a minute or two later clutching several sheets of paper.

'My decree absolute, amongst other things.' He handed the papers to the detective. 'I hope you weren't thinking of charging me with bigamy.'

'No.' The detective was staring at the paper. 'This is dated just over five years ago.'

'You'll find it's the day before I married Kathryn here.'

'Preliminary findings suggest that Jillian Mercer has been dead a little longer than five years.'

'Perhaps you'd better continue your investigations a little longer,' Sean said mildly. 'Call in the kind of forensic experts you chaps have available these days.'

'We intend to.' The police officers exchanged a glance that Kathryn found alarming. Their next words were even more chilling. 'Don't leave town without informing us, will you, Dr Mercer? We'll need to talk to you again.'

Perhaps the most chilling aspect of the unexpected visit was the smile on Sean's face when Kathryn returned to the lounge, having shown the police officers out.

'That was a bit of a surprise, wasn't it? Been rather an eventful day all round, hasn't it, Kathryn?'

'Yes.'

'What do you think about all that?'

'I don't know what to think, Sean. I feel sorry for Jillian.'

'Oh, I wouldn't waste your sympathy.' Sean rattled the ice in the bottom of his glass. 'I suspect she got what she deserved.'

'Nobody deserves to get murdered.'

'Who said she *was* murdered?'

Kathryn was silent. Why had Jillian deserved to die? Because she had walked out of her marriage to Sean? Fear spread tentacles that clutched at her from within. Tentacles that tightened sharply when she heard Sean's chuckle.

'I think it's time we had a little chat, Kathryn.'

'What about, Sean?'

The heavy crystal tumbler, hurled by Sean, hit the front of the drinks cabinet with an explosion of glass that echoed in Kathryn's head as silence fell again. The cloying scent from a bunch of lilies filled her nostrils as she tried to take a steadying breath.

'Oh…let's see.' Sean was pacing now. Rubbing the fingers of his left hand together as though requesting some kind of payment. He moved back and forth across the room, as though delivering a performance on a stage. Then he stopped and waited. Kathryn knew he would wait until she made eye contact and that the longer he had to wait, the fiercer his anger would become. Looking up was a protective reflex. What she saw in his face was enough for her breath to catch.

'I know.' Sean smiled. 'Let's talk about your plans for leaving me, shall we?'

CHAPTER NINE

IT HAD to be done.

The only source of light at the end of a terrifyingly dark tunnel depended on it, but Kathryn didn't know whether she was capable of doing it. It was her only chance. *Their* only chance. But the possibility that it could go horribly wrong was very real and the most heartbreaking aspect of it all was that even if she was about to destroy what mattered most to her, she had absolutely no choice.

They all assumed that she looked the way she did because of her mother's death and, of course, Kathryn accepted the alibi with relief.

'You look fair trauchled, hen,' Mrs McKendry said with obvious concern. 'Are you sure you should be back here again so soon?'

'Yeah. You don't look good.' Stick's pockmarked face creased rather appealingly as he frowned at Kathryn. 'They didn't *expect* you to be back on deck today, did they?'

'I want to be here,' Kathryn assured her colleagues quietly. 'I'd much rather be here than sitting at home.' She avoided Tim's gaze, knowing that he would interpret the statement far too accurately. 'It's better to be busy,' she added hurriedly. 'And I'm fine...honestly.'

'You're not really fine, are you?' Tim had to wait until they were on their way to their first call before he had any time alone with Kathryn. 'You're as pale as a ghost and you've got black smudges all around your eyes. You look...awful, hon.'

'Gee, thanks.' Kathryn summoned a smile. 'I missed a bit of sleep last night, that's all.'

Make that any sleep at all. Behind the locked door of her bedroom, Kathryn had spent the night desperately seeking an alternative to the only course of action that seemed available.

She had found none.

'You didn't answer my texts.'

'My phone died. I had it in the bathroom with me and it fell in the bath.'

'Oh?'

He knew she was lying. The look Kathryn received was a mirror image of the one he'd given her that night when she'd tried to cover up the cause of the bruising on her arm. Would he also make the next logical extrapolation and realise that this lie had something to do with Sean?

Kathryn gritted her teeth and pretended to search for a pen, which she could see perfectly well sitting under the tourniquet and packet of mints on the dashboard. Of course Tim would know she was lying. It had only been yesterday that she'd told him she never let her phone out of her sight and that her ability to communicate with him had been the only thing that had got her through the last few days. The lie was hurting herself as well as Tim. It was a blatant slap in the face considering the trust they had built between them. Kathryn wasn't at all surprised to hear the edge of anger in Tim's tone when he spoke again.

'I didn't sleep that well myself,' he said tightly. 'With worrying about you. There's a phone service place near the hospital. We could drop your phone in after this job.'

'I forgot to bring it.' Kathryn tried to sound annoyed at herself. 'I'll try and remember tomorrow.'

The silence sat there long enough for Kathryn to realise

she had been given a second chance and she had chosen not to take it. Tim cleared his throat.

'How were things last night?' He sounded oddly polite now. 'At home, I mean.'

'OK.' Kathryn pretended preoccupation, reaching for the clipboard with the patient report form. 'Pretty normal, surprisingly.'

She took advantage of the now expected silence to start filling in what she could of the paperwork, like the date and location they were heading for. The call on the vehicle's radio came just as she filled in the spaces for crew names.

'Control to Inglewood 950.'

Kathryn reached for the microphone. 'Nine-fifty. Go ahead.'

'Cancel, cancel,' the voice instructed. 'Stand by for a priority-one call.'

'Roger.'

The radio crackled again within seconds. 'P1 response to 86 Greystone Drive, Kilburnie.'

'Copy that,' Kathryn said. Tim had activated the beacons and she could feel the speed of the vehicle increasing rapidly. 'Nature of call?'

'Burns. Call coming through on your pagers now.'

'Roger.' Kathryn ripped off the report form on the clipboard and scribbled the details of the new location on a fresh form before reaching for the map. Tim switched on the siren now that there was no need for further radio communication.

'Take a left at the top of Wilson Road,' she directed Tim. 'Greystone Drive is second on the left off Maitland Street.'

'Cool.' Tim flipped the siren wail to the high-pitched yelp, with no effect on the slow-moving car in front of them. He leaned on the air horn then and Kathryn could almost feel the alarmed jump of the driver who swerved to the left and clipped a parked car in his hurry to co-operate.

'Oops!' Kathryn bit her lip. It wasn't that uncommon to see minor accidents caused as a flow-on effect of a priority-one response. Tim would normally have expressed sympathy for the unfortunate motorists who would now have to deal with insurance companies and panelbeaters, but the grim expression on his face right now matched his total lack of response to Kathryn's acknowledgement of the mishap. He even leaned on the horn again to hurry the line of traffic ahead, although they were all beginning to pull to the side of the road.

Kathryn felt the knot of tension in her stomach tighten into a painful cramp. It had begun. Tim knew he was being shut out and he wasn't happy. He would be a lot less happy before much longer, but Kathryn couldn't afford to think about this from Tim's point of view. She was doing this because she had no choice. She could only hope that one day Tim would understand…and forgive her.

The burns patient was critical. He had used an accelerant to start his large bonfire and had then tripped and fallen into it in his panic to get clear. It had been too long before his neighbour had heard his screams and got close enough to pull him to safety and even longer before he'd been able to douse the flames on the burning clothing.

'Stay there and keep the hose running for us,' Tim told the neighbour.

'Airway's open. Breathing's rapid and shallow,' Kathryn noted aloud. 'Singed nostrils.'

'Try an OP airway,' Tim instructed. 'He's probably unresponsive enough to tolerate it. Use a bag mask and IPPV with high-flow oxygen.'

Clothing had been cut away and the extensive, full-thickness burns cooled by the time they had their patient loaded only a few minutes later.

'I'll drive,' Tim stated. 'Assist his respirations and don't worry about trying to get any more vital sign measurements for the moment. Back-up is on the way. We should meet them before we get much further.'

Having extra crew members made the pre-hospital emergency care of their patient much more effective, but it was the first time Tim had chosen to continue the driving rather than be in the back with the patient in a situation like this. Kathryn found herself watching Bruce Stanton and her old classmate Jo continuing the care.

'Blood pressure's 98 on 60. Pulse 130.'

'Let's get another dressing on that arm.' Bruce was hanging a new bag of IV fluid but he kept an eye on Jo as she placed sterile dressings to separate the man's charred fingers. 'Good job.' He nodded.

Kathryn could only watch, sitting at the head of the stretcher and still assisting the patient's respirations by squeezing the bag mask each time he breathed in. She saw the look that passed between Jo and Bruce and felt glad that their problems in working together had clearly been resolved.

Ironic, really, when she was creating problems with her own partner that she couldn't allow to be resolved. So far, events were conspiring to assist her reaching her unwelcome goal. The busier they were and the more people around them, the easier it was going to be to push Tim away.

Hopefully, far enough away to reach safety.

The air horn was satisfyingly loud. Kat's totally uncharacteristic lack of reaction to the various responses of fear, apology or outright anger he was sparking only added to the numbness growing from the depths of his despair.

All the other drivers had to do was get out of his way to solve their immediate problem. Tim could see no way to resolve his.

Two days, a night and now a second night of working closely with a woman who had turned into some kind of emotional zombie was becoming unbearable. A woman he loved, dammit, and she wasn't letting him within touching distance. Emotionally or physically. Kathryn's withdrawal had been understandable that first day back. It had been only the day after her mother's funeral. She had clearly needed space and Tim had been only too happy to provide it. She had needed the distraction of being busy and she had received it, by the spadeful.

The second day shift had been incredibly busy as well but Tim had made more of an effort to try and get Kathryn to talk to him. Really talk to him—not just professional exchanges about their patients or shallow conversations about the awful weather. Kathryn was astonishingly adept at avoiding him. She could change the subject before he even realised it was happening. Could move out of reach just before he realised he had intended touching her. She had even managed to avoid any time alone that provided potential privacy, such as sharing the task of collecting supplies from the storeroom.

Last night had been unusually quiet, with no calls coming in after midnight. A perfect opportunity to talk quietly in the comfort of the commonroom with the Green Watch fire crew soundly asleep upstairs, but Kathryn had pleaded tiredness and gone up to her room without even the customary mug of hot chocolate and Tim hadn't seen her again until crew changeover time after 6.30 a.m. There had been far too many people around then, of course, drawn like bees to a honeypot by the smell of the bacon and eggs Mrs Mack had been whipping up for them all.

Well, Tim had had enough. Something was going on and he didn't like it. And as soon as they finished this job he was going to do something about it. If he didn't find out what was going on tonight then they'd be into their four days off and Tim wasn't going to spend that time agonising over what was happening with the prospect that things would be even worse when they were back in close contact again. Anger had been building ever since Kathryn had lied about her phone, but Tim had got past waiting for her to clear the air. Clearly he was going to have to take charge of this himself and he was in just the mood to do precisely that.

Pulling into the driveway of the rest home they had been despatched to, he jammed on his brakes, hoping to get a reaction from Kathryn. She jerked forward against her safety belt but said nothing. Tim got out and slammed his door. He walked straight into the door of the building without waiting for Kathryn to catch him up and leaving her to carry both the resuscitation kit and the life pack.

She didn't catch up until he was in the room of the patient they had been called to see.

'You can put the kit back,' Tim told her. 'Get the paperwork for a life extinct form instead.'

They were far too late to help the elderly resident. Tim attached the leads of the life pack to record the lack of any cardiac activity. He listened with his stethoscope to confirm the lack of any respiratory effort. He noted the cold temperature and fixed, dilated pupils of the patient.

'He's been dead for quite a while.'

'The aide thought he was just asleep. She didn't think tc check for a pulse.'

'Have you got a GP that can come in and sign the deatl certificate?'

'She's on her way.' The rest-home manager sighed. 'Sc are the relatives. It's such a shame. I mean, it was hardl unexpected in a ninety-year-old with such a collection o medical problems, but Arnie was a real favourite around here.'

More than one member of staff could be seen shedding a tear in the kitchen as Tim and Kathryn headed away a short time later. Their grief touched Tim only slightly. He had other things on his mind right now.

'My turn to drive, isn't it?'

'I'll drive.' Tim swung himself into his seat. There was no way he was letting Kathryn into the driver's seat right now. In more ways than one.

'Where on earth are we going?' Kathryn queried when Tim turned off the road well before the suburb of Inglewood.

'This is a local park,' Tim informed her. 'There's tennis courts and a couple of football fields. I used to come here on Saturday mornings as a kid to play rugby.'

'And there's a reason for coming in here in the middle of the night?'

'Yep.' Tim turned into a deserted parking area behind the tennis club rooms. He stopped the ambulance, pulled on the handbrake and cut the engine. Then he turned to Kathryn. 'You've been avoiding talking to me for days. Even when we've had the chance to be together and talk, you've found something else to do. I've done my best to allow you any space you've needed, but it's getting way past being tolerable, Kat. I know you're in a tough space right now but you're shutting me out. Considering how we feel about each other, it's not a pleasant way to be treated and I simply don't understand why you're doing it.' His gaze pinned Kathryn's. 'So tell me.'

'You can't do this, Tim. We're on duty.' Kathryn's face was pale. She looked scared.

'I happen to think this is more important,' he said calmly. 'What's going on, Kat?'

'Nothing.' Kathryn sounded nervous. 'I'm tired, Tim, that's all. Really tired. It's all too much for me. This job… Mum dying.'

He could see the pain in her face as she looked away from him. Then she seemed to gather herself as though what she was about to say needed courage.

'Us,' she added brokenly. 'It's too much, Tim. It's doing my head in.'

'I understand,' Tim said softly. He reached out and touched Kathryn's cheek, and she flinched. Tim swore under his breath as he felt the kick in his guts. 'I only want to help.'

'You can't,' Kathryn said flatly. She still looked worryingly pale and there was a very uncharacteristic air of defeat about her, the way she kept her head bowed like that. 'You're part of the problem, Tim.'

The sudden constriction in Tim's throat made swallowing very difficult. 'What the hell is that supposed to mean?'

'It's…it's not going to happen.' Kathryn's voice was no more than a whisper.

'What's not going to happen?'

'Us.'

Tim's snort was incredulous. 'Too late, babe,' he said softly. 'Newsflash—it's already happened.'

Their night together had sealed their future as far as Tim was concerned. He'd cradled Kathryn in his arms when she'd cried. She never cried. And they had been tears of happiness, not pain or sorrow. Happiness that had been created by the act of physical love. By *him.*

There was no hint of that happiness in Kathryn's eyes now when they met his for the briefest glance. Pain and sorrow were only too evident.

'It can't happen again, then. It's over, Tim. It has to stop.'

'You're *joking*, right?' Unable to stop himself, Tim reached for her hand. 'I love you, Kat.'

There was no answering squeeze on his hand. 'I'll always love you.' He tried to quell the note of desperation he could feel creeping into his voice. 'You do believe that, don't you?'

Still there was no flicker of movement in the hand he was holding. It felt dead. Kathryn's white face in the pale glow of the car-park lighting looked equally lifeless.

'This isn't you talking, hon,' Tim said firmly. He shook his head to try and disperse an odd buzzing sensation. 'Has Sean threatened you in some way?'

'No.' Kathryn's hand moved finally but it wasn't to reassure Tim that his touch was welcome. The message he got as she withdrew her hand was very different.

'You don't have to stay with him a minute longer, Kat. You can come home with me when this shift is finished. I won't let him hurt you.'

'I'm not going to go home with you, Tim. I'm not leaving Sean.'

The buzzing sound got louder. 'You mean right now or… never?'

Kathryn was silent.

'You don't love him.' Tim couldn't keep the desperation out of his tone now. 'Where the hell is this coming from?'

'Relationships are complicated, Tim. You can't judge them from outside. Sometimes it's hard to judge them even from inside. Things have changed in the last few days.'

'Obviously.' Tim sat back. He shook his head. He ran stiff fingers through his hair and then shook his head again. Finally he turned to stare at Kathryn and at that moment their pagers sounded.

'It's a priority one,' Kathryn said seconds later. 'Chest pain.'

Tim didn't move a muscle. 'You're not really married to Sean, Kat. It's not complicated at all. How can you plan to stay with a man you've never even had sex with?'

Kathryn was still staring at the paging device she held in her hand. 'I owe you a great deal, Tim. If my marriage is going to work now, it'll be because of you. You...' She cleared her throat but her next words still sounded rough. 'You...cured me.'

The buzzing had spread. Tendrils of pure ice were shooting right through Tim's body. 'You haven't...*slept* with Sean, have you?'

Again, Kathryn remained silent. Their pagers buzzed again and they both ignored the sound.

'I don't believe it,' Tim said flatly. 'How could you? Did our night together mean that little to you?'

'It meant a great deal.' Kathryn finally looked at him now, her eyes shining with what looked like tears. 'It was a new beginning for me, Tim. The start of a new life.'

'With *Sean*?' Disbelief warred with bitterness.

'It has to be with Sean. He's my husband. I can't break the vows I made. I'm...sorry, Tim. I'm really sorry.'

The voice of the despatch officer at Control seemed incongruously cheerful. 'Inglewood 950. Are you responding?'

Tim snorted. 'I can't accept this. I *won't* accept it.'

'You'll have to.' Kathryn leaned forward and pushed the 'responding' button on the console.

'You really expect me to, don't you?' Bitterness was evolving into anger. 'You think you can just dump me and I'll accept it? Keep *working* with you?'

'I don't expect you to keep working with me,' Kathryn said. 'I'm resigning, Tim. This is my last night at Inglewood. My last night as a paramedic.'

'You're dumping me *and* the job?'

'I have to.'

'Why? Because Sean told you to?' Something didn't ring true about any of this, but Tim couldn't think straight. He was too upset. Angry and afraid. 'Has he threatened you?'

'I've already told you that he hasn't.' Kathryn held up her pager. 'We have to respond to this. It's priority one, in case you hadn't noticed. Someone's life could be in danger.'

Tim's life was in danger. He was dying here and he couldn't detect any hope of immediate resuscitation. 'Is that all you're going to say? That's *it*? Thanks but, no, thanks?'

Kathryn's silence answered nothing but it felt like it was answering far too much. Tim flicked on the beacons and released the handbrake with an angry snap. Gravel sprayed from behind the wheels as Tim accelerated.

The unexpected obstacle of a car blocking the entranceway to the park at this time of night was the last straw. Tim turned on the siren to tell the driver of the silver Range Rover that he'd better get out of their way pretty damned fast.

He didn't need the siren at this time of night in the city streets but he left it on anyway. Something had to fill the unbearable silence between him and his partner. Or should that be *ex*-partner?

The anxious wife of the man with cardiac chest pain was clearly intimidated by the ultra-professional, snappy tone she received on opening her front door.

'I'm Tim. This is Kathryn. Where's the patient?'

'In bed.' The elderly woman stared at Tim and then at Kathryn. Her hand fluttered to her mouth, as though the sight of two stony-faced paramedics had just made her realise how serious this situation was. 'This way.'

'Does he have a history of cardiac problems?'

'Only a bit of angina.'

'Has he used his GTN spray?'

'Yes. Several times. He said it's given him a terrible headache and he feels dizzy.'

'What medications is he on?' Tim wasn't allowing any time for Kathryn to say a thing. From the corner of his eye he saw her place the life pack on the end of the bed and start to uncoil the lead wires, but Tim wasn't about to give her the satisfaction of taking any initiative.

'Get some oxygen on, please, Kathryn. Ten litres a minute via a high concentration mask.'

She complied without even a glance in his direction. *Why was she doing this to him? And why, in God's name, had he given her the power to destroy him like this?*

'Tell me about this chest pain, sir.' Tim wasn't about to allow his own pain to interfere with the way he did his job. This patient, in fact, was going to get the best possible pre-hospital care for his potential heart attack that Tim was able to provide.

Kathryn said nothing other than reporting vital sign measurements or reading out the drug name and expiry date of the medications she was ordered to draw up. The ST elevation on the cardiac trace suggested a barn-door infarct and the protocol was simple to adhere to. The eighty-three-year-old man received oxygen and GTN, aspirin, morphine and metaclopramide. He was placed in a semi-recumbent position on a stretcher and transported expeditiously to the emergency department.

Tim stayed in the back with the patient and his wife, filled in all the paperwork and dealt with the handover to the triage nurse in Emergency. Kathryn drove, held the foot end of the stretcher on arrival and tidied up the vehicle after the job. It was the kind of assistance any probationary officer could provide, but why should Tim worry about any job satisfaction she might be getting? She wasn't even planning to stick at being a paramedic, was she?

And that was almost as unbelievable as her telling him they had no future together. It was all a lie but whatever was going on to cause it, the fact that Kathryn couldn't trust him enough to tell him the truth cast black clouds over the future Tim had been envisaging. It made him doubt that Kathryn did actually love him with anything like the passion he felt for her. And it *hurt*, dammit.

It hurt like hell.

Tim glared at Kathryn as he emerged from the emergency department, leapt lightly down from the loading platform and marched along the side of the ambulance to get into the passenger seat. He slammed the door, put his safety belt on and then pretended total preoccupation in putting a fresh patient report form onto the clipboard and scribbling in the standard details.

Kathryn closed the back doors of the vehicle and slid into the driver's seat. She picked up the microphone.

'Inglewood 950 to Control.'

'Go ahead, 950.'

'We're available at the hospital.'

'Return to station.'

'Roger.'

She drove in silence for several minutes. In a silence laden with the misery she had created.

She hadn't planned on being so cruel. Where had that come from? That horrible suggestion that Tim had solved her sexual problems so that she could now have a 'real' marriage to Sean? It had seemed like inspiration at the time. It had taken her days to screw up her courage to do what she had to do, and the solution had apparently been handed to her on a plate. Something that would be totally effective in reaching the goal she had to reach.

It had been totally effective.

And Kathryn couldn't bear it.

Without bothering to indicate, Kathryn swerved towards the side of the road and brought the ambulance to an abrupt halt.

'I can't do this,' she announced.

'Then get out,' Tim responded coolly. '*I'll* drive.'

Kathryn didn't move. 'I'm not talking about the driving.' She turned her head to find Tim staring at her, his expression unreadable. For the first time in days she found she could hold his glance. She couldn't possibly have looked away, in fact. 'I was lying to you, Tim.'

'I know that.' Tim's lips were dead straight but the faintest hint of a smile lurked in his dark eyes, 'You're a lousy liar, Kat. Far worse than me.'

Her own smile was shaky. Relief coursed through her. Thank God, he had stopped calling her Kathryn.

'I was trying to keep you safe, Tim. It seemed to be the only way.' Once started, the words just spilled out in a rush. 'But I'm not strong enough. I *can't* do this by myself and I can't wait for however long it's going to take before I can find out whether it *has* worked and...and I don't even know if it *will* work, so—'

'Whoa!' Tim held up his hand. 'You've lost me, babe. Back up and start again.'

'I don't know *where* to start.' It wasn't relief making Kathryn shake now. 'The last few days have been a nightmare, Tim. I've needed you so much and I couldn't tell you. I've been trying and trying to find a way out and I can't. Not one that I can live with. One that would keep you safe.'

Tim's eyebrows had been rising steadily. 'Why am *I* not safe?'

'Because Sean is going to kill you.'

And with that, Kathryn burst into tears.

CHAPTER TEN

FINALLY, she had done the right thing.

There was so much comfort to be found within the tight circle of Tim's arms. The touch of his lips on her hair. The soothing words that finally penetrated the sound of her own sobbing and calmed the dreadful tremors that had claimed her muscles. Of course she couldn't have faced this on her own. She wasn't a whole person unless she was with Tim. She could feel his strength flowing into her now.

Raising her head, Kathryn realised with astonishment that they weren't sitting in the front seats of the ambulance in full view of anyone driving past. Somehow Tim had pulled her into the back and his strength was such that she hadn't even realised she was still standing. Her whole weight had been supported effortlessly as she had clung to Tim and released some of the fear and anguish that had been building for so long.

Now Tim eased her into a sitting position on one of the stretchers. He didn't let go of her, thank goodness, but he managed to extract the box of tissues from an overhead locker as he moved.

'Blow your nose, sweetheart,' he said gently. 'It's OK. Sean's not going to hurt you again. And there's no way he's going to kill me. He might be a bastard but he's not a murderer.'

'But he *is*!' Kathryn blew her nose and then sniffed. 'He killed his first wife.'

'What?'

'They've just found her body. The police came to see

Sean the day of Mum's funeral. Just after I got home after I'd been talking to you.'

'He's been arrested? For *murder*? Oh, my God!' Tim pulled Kathryn into his arms again but she pulled back far enough to see his face.

'They don't know it's murder yet. Someone found her body in the bush up the back of the Rimutaka Ranges. It's suspicious but they've got no proof. They won't find any proof either.'

'Why not?'

'Sean said they wouldn't.'

'He's *admitted* murdering her?'

'No.' Kathryn shook her head. 'But I *know* he did. I saw his face, Tim. After the police left he said he wanted to talk to me. About...about any plans I might have for leaving him. He said that if I tried, I might find myself lying in the bush somewhere but...but that it wouldn't be before he dealt with you.'

She let Tim pull her close against his chest as another sob broke free. For a few seconds Kathryn allowed the steady beat of his heart beneath her cheek to be the only thing she was aware of.

'And this morning...' Kathryn had to take a gulp of air before she continued. 'There was this article in the newspaper where a man had taken a gun and gone and shot his ex-wife and their three children...'

'I saw that,' Tim murmured. 'It was horrific.'

'Well, Sean saw me reading it and he leaned over my shoulder and said, "Look at that—some guy's shot his ex-wife. I wonder why?"' Her voice mimicked the sing-song quality that had frightened her so deeply, and Tim's arms tightened protectively.

'Why didn't you come to me, love? How could you have stayed in the same house with such a monster?'

'If I'd left, the only place I could have gone was to you. And if I'd gone to you, I would have put you in danger. The threat is real, Tim. Maybe Sean isn't the murderer, which is why he's so confident he won't get caught. Things can be arranged to be done by other people, you know. Especially when money isn't a problem.'

'You mean you stayed somewhere where you must have been afraid for your own life just so that you could protect *me*?'

Kathryn nodded. 'I know how to deal with Sean. You just have to let him think he's in control. Never criticise him. Tell him how clever he is. I convinced him there's nothing going on. I promised to resign from my job as soon as these shifts were over. I promised to go to the IVF clinic with him and pretended that a baby was all I really wanted.'

'And that crap about there being no future for us? Was that part of some plan you had?'

Kathryn nodded. 'I thought that if there *was* really nothing going on and Sean believed it, I could find some way of leaving him that wouldn't implicate you, and that if I waited long enough after that, we could be together but he wouldn't be able to blame you so you would be safe.' Her smile felt wobbly. 'I was scared, though. I knew I couldn't tell you the truth because I knew you wouldn't go along with the plan.'

'Damn right I wouldn't. Your plan sucked, babe.'

'And even if it had worked, I had no guarantee that you would still feel the same way when I *did* finally tell you the truth.'

'I would always feel the same way,' Tim assured her. 'But I'm bloody glad you didn't make me suffer for that long. The last few days haven't been great for me either.'

'I know. I'm so sorry, Tim.'

'It's OK.' Tim cupped her chin and planted a soft kiss

on her lips. 'We'll get through this, hon. You won't have to even *see* Sean again if you don't want to. I promise.'

'But then he'll *know*. We'll both be in danger.'

'I suspect he knows already.' Tim was staring over Kathryn's head through the side window of the ambulance.

'What?'

'Did you see that car that just crawled past?'

'No. Why?'

'It was a silver Range Rover. It has to be the same one that was blocking us when we drove out of the park earlier. I was too upset to make the connection then but I've just remembered something else.'

Kathryn widened her eyes as words failed her. She had seen a silver car quite recently herself. One had pulled into that parking space close to her when she'd been talking to Tim on the top of Mount Victoria.

'My neighbour dropped in yesterday when he was taking his dog for a walk. He said I was becoming very popular. I asked him why and he said that some good-looking blond chick had asked for directions to my place a few days ago, and right after that some guy in a Range Rover had asked exactly the same question.'

Tim looked more serious than Kathryn had ever seen him look. 'Sean's had you followed, Kat. Probably by some private detective. You can't possibly go home again. I won't let you.'

He ran a hand through his hair. 'I can't believe you've actually been in the same house as him all this time. You're right. He's mad enough to employ someone else to do any kind of dirty work. You're in danger.'

'Then so are you.' Kathryn clutched at Tim's hand. 'What will we do?'

'We'll go to the police and tell them everything. Maybe they won't have enough evidence to arrest him for murder but he won't dare have anything happen to either of us while they're watching him. And they will be watching him very carefully after we've spoken to them.'

Kathryn actually smiled. Stretching out her arm, she allowed herself the luxury of running her fingers lightly over the beloved features of the man beside her. 'I love you,' she whispered. 'And your plan is heaps better than mine was.'

Tim caught her fingers and kissed them. 'You'd better believe it, babe. And don't you dare ever have any plans that don't include me from now on.'

'I won't,' Kathryn promised fervently.

'Shall we go, then?'

'To the police station?'

'Of course.'

The crackle of the radio as they moved towards the front of the vehicle reminded them that their shift still had several hours to run.

'Inglewood 950. Stand by for a priority-one call.'

Tim frowned as he reached for the microphone. 'Anyone else available for this call?' he queried. 'We've got a slight problem that needs dealing with.'

Kathryn smiled wryly as she climbed into the passenger seat. Even with Tim on her side, there was no way Sean could be considered only a 'slight' problem.

'Priority-one call in your patch.' The dispatcher didn't sound remotely interested in any reason they might have for being unavailable. 'Can you respond, 950?'

It didn't matter if there were other vehicles available. They were clearly the closest to the incident and the call was urgent. Tim glanced at Kathryn and she nodded.

'We'll have to do it, Tim. We can go to the police later.'

Tim pressed the microphone button again. 'Nine-fifty responding,' he said. 'What's the address?'

* * *

Five minutes later, they located at an address in a new subdivision set on a steep hillside off the northern motorway.

'I've never been here before.' Kathryn eyed the tall trees completely surrounding the small ultra-modern dwelling. 'It looks like this suburb has just been carved out of a pine forest.'

'Feels like it, too.' Tim reached for the hand-held radio in its charger behind the driver's seat. 'We were lucky to get the truck up that driveway.'

Kathryn collected the life pack and the portable oxygen. Tim picked up the kit. Their boots crunched on rough shingle as they walked towards the front door of the house.

'It's very new,' she commented. 'They haven't even started the landscaping yet.'

'Doesn't do much for me,' Tim responded. 'Corrugated iron should be used for building barns, not houses.'

The front door was open a few inches but Tim knocked anyway. 'Hello,' he called. 'Ambulance here.'

The silence was absolute. Kathryn found herself glancing warily over her shoulder. The road seemed a long way down the hillside. The hallway of the house was as dark as the tree-covered slopes around them, and the beams of light from their torches seemed suddenly pathetic.

Tim pushed the door open further. 'Hello,' he called more loudly. 'Can anyone hear me?'

A faint glow could be seen now from the end of the hallway. Tim stepped through the door.

'Ambulance,' he called again. He turned towards Kathryn before he moved off down the hall. 'Stay behind me,' he said quietly. Then he smiled. 'Just in case.'

He could feel it, too, Kathryn decided. That instinct that something just wasn't right. The feeling got stronger as they moved towards what turned out to be a room lit by only a single lamp. The furniture was sparse and the single wooden dining chair beside the lamp looked out of place amidst a sofa and armchairs. The room was tidy to the point of being weird. Artwork decorated the walls but everywhere else was curiously bare. There were no ornaments or books or even a magazine that might indicate someone was in residence.

'I don't like this,' Kathryn said quietly. 'It's weird.'

Before Tim could answer, they both heard the front door slam. Tim reached for the radio clipped to his belt. He was raising it to his mouth as a figure filled the doorway they had just come through.

'I wouldn't do that, if I were you,' Sean Mercer told him. 'Not if you want Kathryn to live.'

The gun Sean was holding was pointed at Kathryn. With each step her husband got closer and Tim was stunned enough to remain frozen until Sean grabbed hold of the plait lying on Kathryn's neck and used it for a vicious tug that pulled her tightly against him. She dropped the equipment she had been holding and the oxygen cylinder hit the wooden floorboards with a sound loud enough to jolt Tim into action. As the cylinder rolled to one side, he started to swing the large kit he held but Sean stepped back, pulling Kathryn with him, pressing the muzzle of the revolver he held against her head. Kathryn's cry of fear prevented Tim completing whatever plan of attack he might have been instinctively following.

'You don't really think you're going to take control, do you?' Sean's laugh was chilling. 'I've planned this far too carefully to allow that. Drop the radio.'

Tim hesitated and Sean pressed the gun hard enough against Kathryn's temple to make her cry out again. She watched in horror as the radio slid from Tim's hand to hit the floorboards.

'Now sit down.' He pointed the gun at Tim now and jerked his head towards the lone wooden chair. 'Over there.'

With a shove that sent Kathryn staggering to one side, Sean moved to stand in front of Tim as he sat down. 'I had to wait until I knew you were available before I called again,' he said. 'I let the first crew they sent just go away thinking no one was at home.'

Sean picked up a coil of rope and threw it at Kathryn. 'Tie him up,' he ordered.

'Don't do this, Sean.' Kathryn's voice shook. 'Please, don't hurt Tim.'

'I won't,' Sean told her. 'Not yet, anyway. He's going to watch what I do to you first.'

'You *bastard*!' Tim launched himself towards Sean but had only started to move when the shot rang out. With a cry of pain Tim fell back onto the chair, his right hand clutching at his left upper arm. Kathryn gasped at the sight of blood staining the white sleeve of his shirt and oozing through his fingers. It was coming from the side of his arm closest to his chest. A few inches or two further to the left and the bullet would have entered his heart. The reality of the danger they were in was enough to paralyse her.

'I thought I told you to tie him up.'

Kathryn's hands were shaking so hard she could barely make them move to coil the rope around Tim. Any kind of knot was impossible.

'You're bloody useless, aren't you?' Sean snapped. He pushed her aside and pulled at the rope himself, looping and tugging the ends with difficulty due to the gun he still held. Kathryn closed her eyes, praying that it wouldn't go off accidentally. She didn't dare try to tackle Sean herself in case she precipitated exactly that scenario.

A crackling sound made her flinch but the noise was coming from the abandoned radio on the floor.

'Inglewood 950. Have you located?'

Had they forgotten to push the button on the console?

'Inglewood 950. Do you copy?'

Sean had finished tying Tim up to his satisfaction. He used a shorter piece to tie Kathryn's hands behind her back and then he pushed her hard enough for her to sprawl onto the sofa. He moved to the doorway and disappeared from sight. Kathryn struggled to a sitting position and then tried to get to her feet, her gaze locked on Tim's. He shook his head in warning and turned his gaze deliberately towards the radio.

Kathryn understood. Tim had been about to talk on the radio when Sean had confronted them. Had he held his finger on the button long enough for control-room staff to hear what was happening? They would send back-up in any case if they failed to get assurance of the crew's safety. It was only a matter of time until help arrived. Sean obviously wasn't going to kill either of them in too much of a hurry or he would have done so already. If they could keep him talking or otherwise occupied for long enough, they could keep themselves alive.

'Your arm's still bleeding,' Kathryn whispered.

'Not for long. The rope's as good as a tourniquet.'

'Shut up!' Sean had entered the room again. He had a bottle of whisky in one hand and a smaller container in the other, along with the gun. Kathryn saw him put the weapon down on a dining table but the action didn't make her feel any safer. The rope cutting into her wrists underlined just how helpless she was.

The radio sounded again. 'Inglewood 950. Do you require assistance?'

'No, they bloody don't,' Sean snarled. He kicked the radio as he walked past, sending it skittering across the floor to disappear under the table.

'Why are you doing this, Sean?' Kathryn forced herself to try and speak normally. 'I've already told you I'm resigning from my job. I thought I was doing what you wanted. That we were going to try and have a baby together.'

'And you think I *believed* you?' Sean was standing in front of Kathryn now. He took a swallow from the bottle he held and then perched himself on the arm of the sofa. 'You told me you weren't sleeping with *him*, too.' His lip curled. 'You're just as much of a slut as Jillian was, aren't you, Kathryn? And I thought there was something different about you.'

He snorted. 'I even liked the fact you were too frigid to have sex with. Silly me.' Sean unscrewed the cap of the small bottle he was holding. 'I've been saving these up,' he said almost cheerfully. 'There's more than enough to do the job.'

'What job?' Kathryn couldn't pretend a calm desire to keep Sean talking. 'What are you talking about, Sean?'

'My pills.' Sean tipped the small bottle towards his palm and shook it. Dozens of tiny pills spilled out. 'Amiltriptyline. I believe it's quite effective. I've already taken mine, Kathryn. Now it's *your* turn.' He turned to smile triumphantly at Tim. 'If *I* can't have her,' he said calmly, 'nobody will.'

Kathryn's mouth went dry as her brain was assaulted by a whirlwind of thoughts. The sight of the tiny tablets had evoked memories of that case she and Tim had dealt with. What was his name? Blake someone. The pale man that had reminded her of Sean. He'd had the same tablets. What had Tim said about the effects of an overdose?

The worst were the cardiac arrhythmias. They could go into a VF arrest or asystole 'just like that'. She could almost hear the snap of Tim's fingers. And they never survived if they went into VF. How many pills would it take to kill *her*? How many had Sean taken already? She was much smaller than Sean so they might work a lot faster.

Kathryn turned a desperate gaze towards Tim. She didn't want to die. Not for a very, very long time. And when she did, she wanted to be cradled in the arms of the man she loved. The man who loved *her*.

Tim looked astonishingly calm, given the situation they were in, but Kathryn had another flash of memory. Was he doing the duck thing and looking calm on the surface while frantically paddling underneath? If she hadn't been so paralysed by fear she would have smiled at the thought. Instead, she kept her eyes glued on Tim as he mimed a spitting action behind Sean's back.

Her head snapped sideways a fraction of a second before the pain exploded in her cheek.

'Stop *looking* at him,' Sean shouted. 'I'm your husband. Look at *me*!'

Kathryn forced herself to comply. If there was some way she could distract Sean, maybe she could buy a little time.

'I'm looking at you, Sean. I'll do whatever you want.'

'Ha!' Sean stirred the pile of pills cupped in his palm with one finger. 'Where have I heard *that* before?'

'I mean it this time. Don't do anything, Sean. It'll only make things worse.'

Sean snorted. 'They can't get any worse, darling. You think I'm going to go to prison so that you and lover-boy can get it together?'

'Why would you go to prison, Sean?'

He didn't answer. Instead, he turned slowly towards Tim, his lip curling in a disgusted sneer. Still he said nothing. His gaze wandered almost casually around the rest of the room.

'Nice house, isn't it?'

Kathryn nodded. She was twisting her hands slowly between her back and the cushions on the sofa. They were twisting slightly more easily than they had. Was the rope coming loose? Time. She had to win a little more time.

'Whose house is it, Sean?'

'Mine, of course.' Sean was staring at Kathryn again, his face curiously blank. 'You didn't think I was using some sleazy motel for my affairs, did you?'

Tim made a sound like a strangled groan that could have been an expression of disgust at this reminder of how much of a sham Kathryn's marriage had been. Sean's eyes narrowed at the sound and then he jerked forward.

'It's time,' he announced. 'Open your mouth, Kathryn.'

'No-o-o!'

Her protest only made it easier for him. She could feel Sean's fingers and palm bruising her lips as he forced the handful of pills into her mouth. She tried to spit them out but her mouth was held viciously closed. And then glass cracked a tooth as the neck of the whisky bottle was rammed home and Sean was pulling her head back by her hair. The spirits ran over her face, into her eyes and mouth and up her nose.

She was choking. Kathryn could feel her mouth emptying as she gagged and coughed and spluttered, but there was no way of telling how many of those pills went down her throat. Some certainly did. The crash she heard from behind Sean a second before his hands retreated only fed her panic.

'There we go.' Sean sounded pleased. 'That wasn't so bad, was it? My turn again.'

Kathryn couldn't see more than a blurred image through the searing pain and watering of her eyes. Sean seemed to be emptying the rest of the container into his own mouth and washing the pills down with more alcohol. He staggered slightly and Kathryn could see a shape on the floor behind him.

She was still gasping. She screwed her eyes shut against the pain and then forced them open again. Tim's chair had overturned and he was lying on the polished floorboards. He was still tied up and he was lying very still. Had he tried so desperately to intervene in Sean's attack that he'd overturned his chair with enough force to knock himself out? The fear that Tim was seriously hurt cut through Kathryn's own terror, changing it to a rage that consumed her.

The emotion was completely without precedent and lent Kathryn a strength she could never have otherwise possessed. The twist and pull at her bonds actually freed her hands this time and then Kathryn was moving. Pushing herself up from the sofa and using a continuation of that same action to shove Sean backwards as hard as she could.

In fact, Sean toppled so easily that Kathryn fell with him. She rolled sideways onto her knees, bracing herself as she tried to catch her breath, knowing that a return attack would be on her at any moment.

But it didn't happen.

Risking a glance, Kathryn saw that Sean still lay where he had fallen. His eyes were shut. The whisky bottle was still in his hand and a dribble of liquid added to the expanding puddle. Kathryn took no more than a split second to take in the impression that Sean was not about to retaliate because her focus was now on the man she crawled towards.

'*Tim.* Oh, God, Tim. Are you OK?'

'Don't worry about me just yet. Put your fingers down your throat, Kat. Get rid of those pills.'

'I don't think I swallowed that many.' Kathryn's hands were pulling at the knots in Tim's rope.

'Just *do* it, Kat!'

And Kathryn did. And then she could concentrate on freeing Tim. Sean lay without moving.

'Your arm!' Kathryn was dismayed to see torn flesh

still bleeding slowly when the rope came off. 'I'll get a dressing.'

'Not yet.' Tim got to his knees and then his feet. 'Get the life pack, Kat.'

She followed his line of vision but she didn't move. 'For Sean?' she gasped. 'You want to *save* Sean?'

Tim's gaze caught hers. 'We have to try,' he said softly. 'You know that. He can't hurt us any more, sweetheart. Never again, I promise.'

Kathryn wasn't at all sure she could believe the words but he was right. They had no choice. She attached the leads.

'VF,' she heard herself report faintly. Seconds later she was holding the paddles to Sean's chest. 'Shocking at 200 joules,' she warned. 'Are you clear?'

'Clear.'

In the short silence that followed, they watched for the interference to settle on the screen to see if the rhythm had changed.

It hadn't.

They could both hear the faint wails of more than one siren in the distance.

'The cavalry's coming,' Tim said. 'Shock again, Kat. I'll tube him.'

'I can't.'

'We have to try. We need to know that we did our best.'

'No...it's not that.' Kathryn's tongue felt thickened. Her vision was blurring. She felt the paddles slip from her fingers. 'I'm all dizzy, Tim.'

She could see the paddles lying there, discarded on the wooden flooring. And then Kathryn could feel Tim's arms reaching for her as the paddles and then the room around them faded into complete darkness.

EPILOGUE

TREE-RIPENED apples hung like crimson jewels on the trees around the hidden glade.

The April afternoon was as perfect as autumn could get. Warm sunshine enhanced the sweet scent of mature fruit and newly mown grass and, remarkably for this particular part of the world, there was not a breath of wind.

People stood among the tree-trunks surrounding the grass of the clearing and the air of expectancy was as ripe as the apples. The faces of these people included many that Kathryn had come to love. Bruce was there. And Cliff and Stick. Mrs McKendry was dressed in her Sunday best with the most extraordinary pillbox hat she must have been treasuring for more than forty years. Jason Halliday had Megan standing a little unsteadily beside him, her tiny hand completely lost in his. Laura stood beside them, a contented smile on her face and the bundle that contained their new son in her arms.

These people had become an extended family for Kathryn in the last few months and they had all been instrumental in helping her put the pieces of her life back together. They had been among her first visitors when she had woken in hospital to find herself on the road to recovery from her enforced drug overdose.

They had been there to support her when Sean had been buried. They had provided even more staunch support when it was discovered that Sean's marriage to her had been bigamous and the family of the wife who hadn't lived long enough to sign any divorce papers had claimed the vast majority of his fortune.

They deserved it, as far as Kathryn was concerned. It went at least a little way towards atoning for what Jillian's family had suffered. Kathryn had never wanted Sean's money. She had only ever sought safety. And love. And she had survived to find that this was exactly what she now had.

Tilting her head, Kathryn found the face she loved most of all right beside her.

Not part of any extended family.

Part of herself.

Tim was her rock. All she could ever need and more than she'd ever dreamed she would find. He gave her the solid base of an unconditional love that would allow Kathryn to become anything she wanted to be. And she would be able to do exactly the same for him. The wash of such deep love prompted Kathryn to touch a gentle fingertip to the tiny old-fashioned red rose that was pinned to Tim's cream shirt above his heart. It matched the flowers in the bouquet Kathryn was holding.

'They're waiting for us, hon.' Tim held out his hand. 'Are you ready?'

Kathryn smiled. 'I feel like I've been ready for this for ever.'

A tiny frown made a crease between Tim's eyebrows. 'Are you sure? I'd hate to think I was rushing you into this. It is only six months since you buried your first husband.'

'Sean was never a real husband,' Kathryn said softly. 'In any way that counts. This was my idea, anyway, and as far as I'm concerned, Tim McGrath, I'm getting married for the first time right now.' She squeezed his hand. 'The first *and* the last time.'

Tim bent his head to touch her lips with his own. His

smile lit his face with the same joy that Kathryn was experiencing.

'OK, then,' he whispered. 'Let's just do it, sweetheart.'

They were both still smiling as they began to move into the dappled sunshine of the glade. The place that had once been a child's refuge and was even more special now because it marked the point from which there had been no turning back from the life Kathryn would have with the man she loved. There couldn't be a better place to declare their love and make the vows that would last a lifetime.

'Yeah.' Kathryn's sigh was a soft sound of pure happiness. 'Let's.'

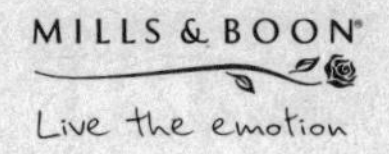

0205/03b

Medical romance™

THE DOCTOR'S PREGNANCY SURPRISE by Kate Hardy

(London City General)

Dr Holly Jones has never recovered from the shock of losing David Neave's baby – nor from the way he disappeared from her life. Years later they find themselves working together in A&E, and as their long-held secrets come bubbling to the surface they begin to renew their very special bond. Until Holly discovers she's pregnant again!

THE CONSULTANT'S SECRET SON *by Joanna Neil*

Dr Allie Russell is managing the best she can – juggling her work in A&E and Search & Rescue with her two-year-old son. Then Nathan Brewster arrives back in her life as the new A&E consultant. He doesn't know he's Matty's father, and Allie wants to keep it that way. But as she and Nathan draw closer again, it's only a matter of time before he discovers the truth!

NURSE IN RECOVERY *by Dianne Drake*

Charge nurse Anna Wells's life has been shattered by an accident. She needs someone very dedicated and special to help her put the pieces back together... someone like brilliant Rehabilitation doctor Mitch Durant. But Mitch is burnt out, the last thing he needs is another patient – until he sees Anna and realises she's a challenge he just has to take on...

On sale 4th March 2005

Available at most branches of WHSmith, Tesco, ASDA, Martins, Borders, Eason, Sainsbury's and all good paperback bookshops.

Visit www.millsandboon.co.uk